828

F23 c

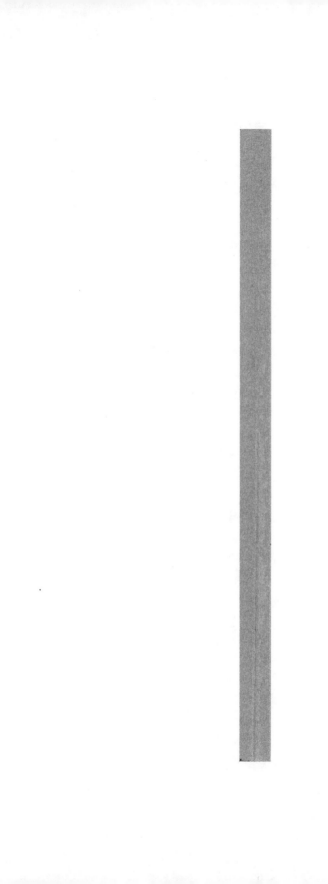

CHARMIAN
LADY VIBART

BY

JEFFERY FARNOL

BOSTON

LITTLE, BROWN, AND COMPANY

1932

To

CHARMIAN JANE

and

SUCH AS DO LOVE HER

Sunnyside, June, 1932

CONTENTS

viii   Contents

CHARMIAN, LADY VIBART

CHAPTER I

"TWENTY-TWO years!" exclaimed Charmian, Lady Vibart, beating petulant white fingers on the windowpane, "twenty-two years — it's preposterous!"

"Eh?" enquired Sir Peter, raising his dark head from the book that engaged him. "I beg your pardon, my dear, but what is preposterous, pray?"

"Everything!" she answered, flashing an angry look at him over rounded shoulder. "You . . . me . . . us! And to-morrow is my birthday!"

"To be sure," he murmured, turning a page. "I have not forgotten; indeed I — "

"And Peter, I shall be forty- . . . forty-two . . . !"

"Three!" he corrected. "Forty-three, to be exact, — though I can hardly believe it, you — wear so well . . . amazing!" Here his gaze went back to his book while Charmian, frowning at the wide, sunny garden and tree-shaded park beyond, rapped quicker and louder than ever, until Sir Peter sighed, stirred and glanced up again.

"My dearest," he murmured, gently reproachful, "if you could contrive to . . . tap a little more softly — "

"My love," she answered, turning to frown at him, "no! Not until you are so extreme obliging to favour me with your attention, — oh, put your hateful book down, Peter — do!"

Sir Peter Vibart laid by the offending tome and surveyed his handsome lady with brow serene as usual and eyes faintly apprehensive.

"Dear soul," said he in murmurous reproof, "though we are in my library and this my customary hour for study, still I am ever ready to break my rule for you as — "

"Rules?" cried Charmian, in sudden blaze of anger, "there it is — custom, rote and rule, — rule, rote and custom! At such an hour we must do this, at such an hour we must do that, but never, oh, never anything worth while!"

"My dear," said Sir Peter, a little dazed, "my dear — "

"Tush!" cried Charmian and stamped at him. "You ride to the markets — like a farmer! You gape at cattle shows — like a drover! You tramp your fields — like a ploughboy! You read your books like a — oh, like a Peter Vibart! And you vegetate like a — hateful cabbage!"

"God bless my soul!" gasped Sir Peter, drooping in his chair.

"And as for me, Peter, I'm breaking my heart, losing my spirit, pining away — fading, Peter! But you, so perfectly content, are blind in your serene self-complacency and never see it, — cannot, will not see it — "

"Good Gad!" he exclaimed and was out of his chair and had his arm about her shapeliness, all in a moment; then, lifting her unwilling head, he looked deep into her unwilling eyes.

"Pining are you, my Charmian?" he questioned tenderly. "Fading away? Then I vow you do it very gracefully — "

"But I am forty-three, Peter — of course I am!" sighed she.

"And I think more beautiful than ever." At this, she condescended to look at him.

"Perhaps you only think so, Peter, because I happen to be yours, and you are so self-assured that any and everything belonging to Sir Peter Vibart is and must be of the very best according to Sir Peter Vibart, seeing Sir Peter Vibart is altogether such a very superlative creature, — such a very grave, sedate, highly respected — gentlemanly personage!"

"I wonder?" said he, beginning to frown.

"Undoubtedly!" she nodded. "And our lives are — wasting away, the years flitting by so dreadfully fast, and what . . . what have you achieved?"

"Yourself!" he answered, smiling. "Our son Richard. Then too, our tenants are prosperous and happy, every farm — "

"Indeed," sighed she, "you grow bovine as the prize cattle you take such a ridiculous pride in! Where are your youthful ambitions? All gone! To-day you are too ineffably content for exertion or anything but a very clodlike country gentleman. Oh, do you wonder I am breaking my poor heart here among all this smug rusticity . . . these miles of well-tilled fields . . . and barns . . . and hayricks — do you?"

"I'm wondering, Charmian, if it would break more comfortably in London among crowded streets and reeking chimney pots?" And now it was Sir Peter who stared so wistfully out into the peaceful, sunny garden and drummed upon the window pane. "Perhaps," said he at last, his tone wistful as his look, "yes, perhaps we . . . I . . . have been too happy. You have made me almost too content, Charmian; I've wanted nothing since our boy came . . . our son Richard —"

"I wanted him named Peter, Peter."

"But agreed he should be called after our dear Sir Richard Anstruther. . . . And, well, dear — Richard is and has been my ambition, you know all my hopes have been centred in him —"

"And yet, Peter, you send him on the Tour with a — a dreamy, small mule of a man, you permit him to wander about the Continent with a bookworm . . . a fool —"

"A fool?" repeated Sir Peter, in shocked accents. "You cannot mean poor Chantrey?"

"I do mean poor Chantrey; the creature's a worm, always in a book, a dotard, a — "

"My dear, Tobias Chantrey is an eminent scholar, a wrangler, a senior prize man — "

"And helpless as a baby!"

"Well, but Richard is a manly fellow and — "

"Only just nineteen, Peter!"

"Precisely! But then Richard is — my son — "

"Your son, sir, oh, yes; but he is mine also, if my memory serves — " Now at this, Peter laughed and, drawing her close, kissed her; but breaking free, she rubbed off the kiss with dainty handkerchief and fronted him sullen-eyed.

"Indeed, Sir Peter, he is your son but despite this inestimable privilege he is not infallible nor immune from the harms and dangers that beset less fortunate youths — simply because he is so blessed as to be sired by — Sir Peter Vibart."

Now at this Peter scowled, then he laughed and, sitting on a corner of his littered and book-strewn desk, surveyed his beautiful wife with darkly bright, questioning eyes.

"Charmian," said he in soft, reverent voice, "we have been married twenty-odd years and, God be thanked, you have proved all and more than I dreamed you. You are so various you might stand for Womanhood's epitome. God made you beautiful but, behind the wonder of your eyes, placed an intellect that makes your carnal beauty divine — almost, for, my dear, you needed mastery. Then my Charmian, He glorified you with Motherhood and I became so humbled, my dear, so awed by the very wonder of you and the ever-growing marvel of our child, that I no longer played the master but gave my mind to lesser things and suffered you to rule until — to-day, it seems . . . why Charmian . . . dear heart . . ." Here his arm swept about her again, for she was sobbing:

"Oh, Peter . . . my dear . . ." she murmured, lovely head snugged against her breast, "I . . . never thought . . . never dreamed you had such thoughts of me . . . nowadays . . . such holy, reverent thoughts . . . after

all these years. My dear, you make me hate myself . . . I feel unworthy such a love, — because I am not . . . oh, never was half so good,
so wonderful as your sweet dream of me —
though Richard is, of course . . . Some day
Rick will be a man like you — honourable and
gentle, my Peter, and brave enough to think
the best of . . . of life and . . . everybody.
But, ah, my dear — hold me tight, Peter —
there is a demon in me . . . there always was
. . . a demon of discontent urging me to do
. . . oh, wild things . . . and sometimes,
Peter, I — do them . . ."

"Of course!" he murmured, kissing her
glossy hair. "Though you never did gallop
your horse up the steps of St. Paul's Cathedral,
twenty-two years ago!"

"No!" said she, nestling closer. "No! But
then I . . . loved to play with fire . . . and
. . . oh, you remember I . . . ran away with
your Cousin Maurice because he was a — a
devil; though — I ran away from him, Peter."

"Yes — to me, dear — thank God! And,
having married me, have lived fairly content
with me all these years, which I esteem very

marvellous, considering you once called me
. . . 'a lamb!' Do you remember?"

"Yes . . . yes!" she answered, in voice between sob and laugh. "And you so mightily indignant, Peter! Yes, I called you a lamb . . .
though you had just driven off a wolf . . . a
demon! So, my Peter, be strong again, tame
me! Drive away my own particular demon that
torments me with these wild fits of restless discontent."

"Dear heart," he murmured, fondling a way-
ward curl at her temple, "what is it troubles
you? Are you grieving for our Richard, —
worrying about him?"

"No . . . yes . . . I don't know," sighed
she, a little breathlessly; "I feel . . . I think
I'm what our Janet would call 'fey' . . . a
feeling of impending evil."

"I know!" said Peter, and kissed her. "And
yet Richard's last letter was very cheerful. But,
dear, I'll recall him at once if —"

"No, Peter, no — it would be foolish of me
to cut short his pleasures for a . . . a whim."

"Then we'll go to Town; the house in St.
James's Square is —"

"Yes, Peter dear, but it is such a vast barracks of a place for just — us two! So many servants everywhere . . . and London will be a howling desolation until the season opens — "

"Hum!" quoth Peter, somewhat hipped. "Well, supposing we run over to Paris for a week or so; the Beverleys are there and — "

"That would be perfectly delightful, dearest, — except for the hateful sea passage."

"But you never mind the sea, Charmian."

"I should — this time, Peter."

"Oh! Then what — "

"Oh, Peter — can't you . . . guess?"

"No, upon my life!" Now at this, Charmian frowned at him, sighed, flushed and, vivid mouth close to his ear, whispered.

"Eh? The old cottage?" he exclaimed. Charmian nodded.

"But my dear," said he, glancing rather furtively round about upon the book-lined walls and luxurious comfort of this spacious chamber, "won't it be rather — damp?"

"Damp?" cried she in choking voice and would have broken from him, but Peter's long arms held her fast.

"And so, Charmian . . . sweetheart, we'll go whenever you will — "

"No!" she cried, struggling passionately. "Not now — "

"Yes," said Peter, squeezing her into submission, "this very day."

"And it is not damp, Peter! You know I've had it preserved . . . cared for, just because it is the dearest old cottage that ever was."

"And the holiest!" he added fervently. "So there we'll go. . . . How good it sounds, Sissinghurst, you and I!"

"Ah, but do you wish to go — truly?" she enquired very wistfully.

"I'll order the horses at once," he answered; "no, we'll order them together — come!" So, hand in hand, forth went they into the sunshine and looking into each other's eyes, the years rolled backward. . . . Charmian's lashes drooped, her lips curved to such tender smile that he caught his breath.

"Oh, Charmian," he murmured, "how entirely lovely you can be — "

"Dear Peter," she sighed, "I am . . . forty-three!"

Walking slowly and very close together they crossed smooth lawns and followed trim paths towards the Home Farm with its wide range of splendidly appointed stable buildings that were the pride (among other things) of Sir Peter's heart.

"Dear old Sissinghurst!" murmured Charmian happily. "And the country round about will be looking glorious."

"Yes," he answered. "And yet Sussex — this home of ours — is lovelier, I think. Look around you, dear, — the old Manor there, our Holm Dene, as Saxon as its name, its foundations rooted deep in South Sex here long before the Conquest, itself growing with succeeding generations. See over there — away to the dim line of woods and blue downland beyond, — now across to the sea, — ours, my Charmian, all ours and a fair heritage for our dear Richard."

"Yes," she sighed, "oh, yes! But then the cottage . . . our cottage, Peter, is in Kent and so I love — " But here he kissed her.

"Horseback, Peter, bridle paths! We should be there by six o'clock; old Mrs. Westly shall make tea for us down in the village — "

"But Janet is no horsewoman, dear — "

"Janet?" repeated my lady, opening her beautiful eyes at him.

"Janet, of course. However, the barouche will hold us all and — "

"Who are 'all', pray?"

"You and Janet, young Mordaunt and myself — "

"But I'm not taking Janet. And what on earth do you want with a private secretary in our cottage?"

"Not in the cottage, dear heart; he will put up at 'The Bull' and — "

"He will — not, Peter! He will remain here and so will Janet."

"But, my dear — "

"We are going — alone, Peter! Just you and I!"

"But Charmian, it so happens I am much pressed with affairs just at present and — "

"No matter — "

"But, my dear soul, it does matter. There are the new buildings at South Dene and Westover and my improvements at Fitworth. And then Abbeymere is making trouble about that pestilent right of way, confound him!"

"And so I am going to take you away from it all, Peter dear. We are going to elope . . . run off with each other!"

"But Charm — "

"So it's all settled!" she nodded. "And I shall ride my Marchioness; she's speedier than your Marquis, as I'll prove." Sir Peter had paused to regard her lovely (though resolute) face and to rub his chin very hard (a habit with him when at any loss) when rose the sound of quick, light footsteps and a young gentleman came hasting to them, a slim-legged, ox-eyed young gentleman who bowed, his large eyes glancing wistfully aside at my lady's vivid and stately beauty.

"What is it, Mordaunt?" enquired Sir Peter.

"Your agent, sir, Mr. Berry, has just ridden in and is urgent to see you."

"Did he say what about, Charles?"

"Nothing to matter, of course!" sighed Charmian. "There never is. Tell him you are busy, Peter."

"Your ladyship's pardon," sighed Mr. Mordaunt, his large eyes eloquent of tender apology. "But Mr. Berry said it was important. He also mentioned something of a warning from the Earl of Abbeymere — "

"That odious creature!" exclaimed Charmian.

"Is Berry at the house?" enquired Sir Peter, glancing thitherwards.

"Yes, sir. He says you made an appointment to — "

"Then, Charles," spake my lady's smooth though compelling voice, "you may tell Mr. Berry Sir Peter and I are going away for — oh, here comes the persistent wretch!"

Heavy boots, jingling spurs, and John Berry, a square, red-faced, hearty man, came striding, dusty from the road and himself full of bustle and business.

"Morning, sir, and your ladyship!" said he, heartily gruff. "Sorry to disturb but — Sir Peter, to-day is Tuesday!"

"Well, Berry, and what then?"

"Sir, you engaged to ride with me to Westover, the new cottages."

"Why, so I did! Those cottages, of course

. . . to decide whether they shall be roofed with thatch or tile."

"That's the point, sir, — tile or thatch."

"I'm inclined to tile them, Berry."

"Tile's more expensive, sir."

"Though to be sure thatch would be less remarkable; all the village is thatched, I believe?"

"Every cottage, sir."

"On the other hand, Berry, tile is more enduring."

"Then," sighed my lady, stifling a very apparent yawn, "roof them with both. And now let us go."

"Begging y'r pardon, my lady," quoth John Berry, with clump and rattle of boots and spurs. "But, Sir Peter, I'm here mainly to say the tenders are in for the new hall you're building at Boscombe, estimates and plans all ready, sir."

"Excellent!" exclaimed Sir Peter. "I'll look over them at once. You have them here?"

"No, sir, seeing we ride to Westover, I left 'em there with the other papers."

"Come, Peter, shall we go?"

"Go where, my dear?"

"To the stables, sir. To order our horses. To ride away together."

"Hum!" quoth Sir Peter, rubbing his chin harder than ever. "Suppose we postpone it until to-morrow? Yes, to-morrow! We will start very early — "

"Begging your pardon, sir," quoth John Berry, boots and spurs in evidence again, "to-morrow is Wednesday!"

"I'm aware of this, John."

"Well, on Wednesday — to-morrow, sir, you've promised to take a look at the new road you're building and then you've arranged very positively to ride with Mr. Vere Manville to look over Squire Golightly's new Highland cattle."

"By George, so I did!" admitted Sir Peter, glancing at his wife's averted face a little uneasily; "you see how it is, my dear?"

"Oh, perfectly!" she murmured. "And my lord and master, I would most humbly crave word with you — in the arbour yonder."

Now here Sir Peter became slightly appre-

hensive as he noted the angle of her stately
head.

"Wait for me at the stables, Berry," said he.

"Very good, Sir Peter. Shall I tell Adam to
have you a horse saddled?"

"Yes, say I'll ride the Marquis. . . . Now,
my dear," said he, drawing Charmian's hand
within his arm. But when they were seated side
by side in the bowery arbour, she was silent so
long that he questioned her at last:

"Well, dear Heart, what is it?"

"Everything!" she sighed. "You, Peter, your
house, your cottages, your tiles and thatch and
cattle . . . our life."

"Why then, Charmian, tell me all about it."

"Tell you?" she repeated, with weary gesture. "That is just the hopelessness of it all —
that I should have to tell you — that you cannot or will not see for yourself."

"See what, my dear, in heaven's name —
what?"

"That you are nothing more than a glorified
farmer, and hatefully content . . . with no
thought or ambition above your crops and
cattle and cottages and things!"

"My dear, surely you are a little unjust to me?"

"You are out all day . . . and every day!"

"Of late . . . well, perhaps I have been . . . these many new ideas and improvements . . . and an estate such as this needs a great deal of care and management—"

"You employ John Berry and others to do this for you."

"Yes, dear, but—"

"You love it, Peter! You only live now for Holm Dene and the estate; it has swallowed you up!"

"Good Gad!" he exclaimed. "All this because I have put off our trip to Sissinghurst!"

"No, not Sissinghurst—not Sissinghurst!" cried she, a little wildly. "To the cottage . . . our cottage! Ah, but you don't or won't understand! Peter . . . Peter . . . how blind you are! How hatefully, odiously prosaic you have become! And how very detestably Peter-Vibartish!"

"I fear I don't apprehend," he answered, rather stiffly.

"No, of course you don't!" she sighed. "You

don't understand yourself — and me not in the least, and poor Richard scarcely at all. No, you are not very wise, Peter, and are becoming even less so."

"Still," he retorted, "I venture to hope and think I am not an absolute fool — "

"Only perhaps in one or two instances," she sighed.

"Indeed? May I know of them?"

"Oh, yes," she answered, sweetly gentle, "I will tell you with pleasure. You are at your most absolute-foolishest in your treatment of our Richard — "

"Of Richard — my treatment — ?" Sir Peter actually gaped.

"Certainly, Peter! You are almost a stranger to him since he grew up."

"Charmian, now what under heaven do you mean?"

"Just this, my poor dear: that as our son has grown in years, you have grown in parental dignity, — so stately and aloof, so lofty and austere, indeed such a remote, Peter-Vibartish, Roman father that, although the poor boy is overawed, of course, you have risen so far beyond him that now he hardly knows you, does not understand you and consequently cannot possibly love you as he should and . . . as I could wish."

"Well! God . . . bless . . . my soul!" exclaimed Sir Peter, and sat staring at the lovely speaker in the most profound astonishment while she, sighing plaintively, gazed wistfully across the sunny park.

"You paint a — a deplorable picture of my fatherhood, Charmian!" said he, at long last.

"I paint you the Vibart parent-male as I see him and Richard experiences him!" she retorted. "I could also paint you the Vibart spouse-male, who will very soon be riding the sunny lanes — not with his wife, alas, — but with a servant on business that servant is paid to do and can probably do a great deal better, but — this is the Vibart way!"

Sir Peter's dark eyes sparkled beneath frowning brows, his lean chin (always somewhat doggedly aggressive) seemed more prominent than usual as, starting to his feet, he seemed about to speak but choked back the words and bowed instead; while she, looking up at him, serenely wistful, smiled faintly.

"Oh, say it, Peter, say it!" she murmured. "Forget your cold austerity and Vibartly dignity and swear at me if you will. I am your meek listener."

"Charmian," said he, in accents gentle as her own, "it is only those we truly love and revere can hurt us most. As for Richard, our son, you know his life is infinitely more to me than my own, that his future is my — well — everything! That my abiding hope and most cherished dream is to see him worthy his heritage and — a greater, better man than I . . . . How cruel, how unjust you are to me your own true heart will tell you . . . and . . . ah, well, this storm-in-a-teacup will soon pass as they all do . . . but such waste of life and sentiment! Meanwhile, since a landlord's first thought should be for his tenantry's welfare, I'll about my business." And with a bow altogether too ceremonious, Sir Peter turned and went.

Charmian sat there, dimpled chin on dimpled fist, staring at vacancy until, roused by footsteps, she glanced up to behold young Mr.

Mordaunt looking down at her with his great, soulful eyes.

"Sir Peter has gone, Charles?" she enquired. "And left a message for me, of course?"

"Yes, madam, he bid me tell you he might be detained."

"He would!" she nodded. "Pray ask Miss Janet to meet me in the pleached walk."

When Mr. Mordaunt had departed, Charmian arose, stepped from the arbour and sighed very distressfully, but there was fire in her eye, resolution in her step and indomitable purpose in every curve of her shapely body.

CHAPTER II

TELLS HOW CHARMIAN WROTE A LETTER AND WHY

FROM this pleached walk, demurely trim as were all walks and paths here at Holm Dene, one might enjoy a prospect of the mansion itself, — a thing of beauty from pre-Norman foundation stones to Elizabethan chimneys. A noble house of ruddy brick, mellowed by weather and time, enriched by carved timbering and bargeboards, roofed mostly with mossy stone, after the Sussex fashion; and yet, despite hoary age, it smiled rejuvenated and, like the wide, undulating park, the trim lawns, paths and hedges, bore mute though eloquent testimony to its owner's loving and tender care.

But just now, leaning back on the marble seat that throned her, Lady Vibart was frowning at it. Now presently as she sat thus in peevish contemplation, upon the warm, still air rose a sound, a clink and clank vaguely martial, that

grew ever louder and more so; a subdued, ring-
ing clash suggestive of meeting swords, bayo-
nets, and foemen's steel in deadly opposition;
which dire sounds heralded the approach of a
tall, somewhat angular, very dignified lady and
were explained by the enormous silver chatelaine she bore girt about her person almost as
it had been an ancestral claymore or broad-
sword, for Miss Janet McFarlane was Scots to
her rigid backbone and so proud of the fact
that she talked as broadly as she knew how,
until at all perturbed, when her speech became
mellifluously English.

"So 'tis there y' are, ma wee birdie!" quoth
she, halting with clash of invisible broad-
swords. "And my certie, 'tis unco fashed ye'll
be, I'm thinkin'. Whaur's it the noo, Charmian-
Sophia?"

"Everything, Janet, — myself, this place —
Peter!"

"Then na doot 'twill be y'r liver! A sup o' my
dandelion tea — "

"Janet, don't be offensive. Sit down! Now, —
look about you. The house, these walks, the
park — everything . . . so detestably orderly

and precise! Not a leaf out of place and the house itself as serenely content as — Peter!"

"Fegs, 'tis a richt bonnie hoose — "

"But oh, Janet, was there ever such a house, my dear? And such shaven lawns! Such soft-footed servants! Such outrageously orderly perfection indoors and out! Such persistent, pervading care of everything and every one! Such overpowering Vibartism! Janet — I could scream!"

"Then do't, ma dearie! Scream awa', m' dear soul, whiles I cut your stay-lace. Then a cup o' my dandelion — "

"Janet, don't be a fool!"

"Eh? A fule is't?"

"Oh, Janet, my dear, I — " the soft voice choked, the deep eyes overflowed at last and swaying to Miss Janet's ready breast, Charmian pillowed her woeful head there as she had done many a time as a motherless child, to be clasped, kissed and cherished very tenderly in two strong, very capable arms.

"My dear, my dear!" sighed Miss Janet, in tone strangely gentle. "My own precious, what troubles you so?"

"P-eter!" sobbed Lady Vibart, giving full vent to her grief.

"But he loves you, dear soul, he loves you dearly."

"Ah, yes, I know this, Janet, — he always will, just as I shall always love him, but . . . his love has changed so . . . he is become so — remote!"

"Tush, my dear! The man worships you with his every breath! I've seen it in his eyes, heard it in his voice. You are the very life of him."

"His life? I wonder! For Janet, you know how I meant to — run off with him to our old cottage. . . . The cottage, Janet! You know how I have planned for it, schemed and lived for it — well, he can't find the time, Janet; he . . . won't!"

"Aweel, the man's only a man, that's all, m' dearie. Forbye a man canna juist see things from a woman's angle, 'specially in love."

"True!" sighed Charmian tearfully. "Quite true, my dear wise Janet; this is why I'm going away."

"Eh? Going? Away? Where to? What for? When?"

"Yes, my dear. To Cambourne, Janet. To rouse him, wake him, shake him! And I'm going to-day."

"No, no — "

"Yes! A thousand times — yes! I'm bitterly resolved, hatefully determined and nothing shall stay me."

"Then I'm coming too!"

"Of course you are."

"But Charmian, oh, my dear, have you thought what you are doing . . . the possible consequences?"

"Fully! Thoroughly, Janet! Are my eyes swelled? Is my poor nose scarlet? Peter is lost in an apathy of content, submerged in a slough of self-satisfaction . . . and there's forceful alliteration for you! My Peter is utterly bogged in a bovine beatitude and needs being awaked with a shock, Janet, — jogged to a proper realization of all that I am to him. And, Janet, I am about to jog him — violently! So come, — come and pack."

And because Miss Janet knew argument to be of none avail, she went, clashing remonstrance at every step. Thereafter, while she

busied herself and my lady's chattering maids
with trunks, hatboxes, etc., Charmian sat down
and indited this letter.

Dear Peter,

Acting on your admirable precept that a
landlord's first thought should be the welfare
of his tenantry, I have hastened to Cambourne,
fired with zeal for mine.

How long it will take you to thatch and tile
all your cottages, build your schools and stare
at cattle and things, this humble person cannot hope to even surmise. But when all such
tremendous matters are settled to your entire
satisfaction (if ever!) pray come and find
again your

solitary wife, lowly subject and
faithful consort — Charmian.

P.S. I shall be at Cambourne in my dear, loved
Kent.

"There, Sir Peter!" quoth she, folding and
sealing this epistle. "Let that stir your dignity!
Rouse, sneeze, yawn but — wake! Oh, Peter,
wake, wake and know — or — dear heaven,
what shall become of me?"

CHAPTER III

Giveth a Brief Glimpse of Valentine, Viscount Iford

THE Norns, those fateful sisters threading ever the warp and weft of human destiny, so contrived that Charmian's carriage, the barouche, should snap the pole in the beauteous neighbourhood of Tenterden, that right pleasant, wide-streeted village. Here then, their vehicle halting for repairs, she and Miss Janet descended before the goodly hospice yclept The White Lion and were ushered therein to cosy chamber by a small, pale, worried-looking man, whose troubled eyes, even while he took their order for refreshment, roved in agitated manner, and who seemed to be listening for other and more dreadful sound.

"Yon man's sick, or — afeart o' something!" quoth Miss Janet, loosing her bonnet strings.

"He certainly had an odd expression, Janet."

"M' dear, he was like an aspen — a' of a quiver and quake!"

"The poor man is undoubtedly in some trouble," my lady agreed. "Let us enquire," and she rang the bell, answered after some delay by the same harassed-seeming person.

"Pray, are you the landlord?" Charmian enquired in her most gracious manner.

"Yes, madam," he answered, glancing apprehensively from door to ceiling.

"You appear to be in some trouble, some distress. Can we help you?"

"Thank you, madam, no . . . no, I — " he checked suddenly and remained staring ceilingwards with horrified eyes, as from the chamber immediately above came the roar of bibulous voices upraised in song.

"Is — that your trouble?" enquired Charmian.

"No, madam, — yes, — that is — "

"Yes — oh, yes, lady!" cried a tearful voice and in upon them ran a woman, her comely middle-aged face haggard and tear-stained. "Up there, my lady!" she sobbed, pointing frantically above her head, "wild gentlemen

from London . . . they've took my maid — my
poor darter — they've got my Pen and they're
a-making of her drunk! Oh, ma'm, they mean
wickedness and no one to stay 'em. Mr. Joyce
here have done his best — "

Charmian arose and with her Miss Janet,
who though she wore no militant-clashing
chatelaine, glared ceilingwards with gray eyes
that held a look suggestive of vengeful steel as
she followed Charmian out of the room and up
the stair.

Reaching a door whence this riotous chorus
proceeded, Charmian flung it wide and stepped
into a room hazy with the reek of tobacco
smoke.

At her sudden appearance, the clamorous
singing quavered to silence, to a breathless
hush, wherein stood Charmian, her stately
form and beautiful, high-bred features eloquent of disdain and abhorrence. Very slowly
and with an almost painful deliberation she
surveyed the three silenced revellers, each in
turn, their flushed faces and disordered attire;
lastly she turned and looked again where at
head of the littered table sat a tall, dark man

who held a faintly struggling girl upon his knee; and with her scornful gaze on this man, Charmian spoke to the half-tipsy girl:

"My poor child, come with me."

"My pretty witch," laughed the dark man, "sit where you are and show Madam Spoilsport how you can kiss."

"Odious animal!" exclaimed Charmian, advancing serenely resolute. "Debased wretch, had I a whip, you should feel it!" and she swept towards them with such majestic wrath that the girl whimpered and the man started afoot.

"Madam," said he thickly, teeth bared in smiling ferocity, "such unmeasured terms I do not permit from man or woman. Stand back then or —" his fierce voice was drowned in the crash of breaking glass and Miss Janet, flourishing a jagged bottle neck, spoke in her turn.

"Sae muckle as lift a hond an' I'll cut the dastard face off ye!"

"Why . . . what . . . what the devil —" stammered the tall, dark man, recoiling. Quoth Charmian imperiously:

"Brutal sot, loose that girl!"

"B' God," cried the man, in paroxysm of fury, "I'll not endure your tongue — "

"You will, Frayne," said a drawling, sleepy voice, "you will endure what you deserve . . . as I shall!" So saying, from high-backed settle beside the hearth rose a fourth reveller; slight of form was he and very youthful-seeming at a glance, for his hair clustered in golden curls, his cheeks, though a little pale, were smooth, but his firm-lipped mouth showed grim and his blue eyes looked between their long lashes with a dreadful weariness that gave innocence the lie direct, — thus mouth and eyes were in sharp and utter contrast with the youthful rest of him.

At sight of Charmian he started, flushed boyishly then, opening his lacklustre eyes, curled his lips in smile of age-old, cynical weariness and bowed.

"Dear Lady Vibart," he murmured, "very unexpected pleasure! I hope I see you in all health. I trust Sir Peter is well and our Richard blooming."

"Iford!" she exclaimed. "Viscount, you —

here! Think shame of your vicious company
and yourself."

"Dear lady, I do, believe me," he answered,
still smiling. "I despise my company utterly
and myself quite heartily — as usual. Frayne is
generally a beast when the bowl is trolled. I
allude to Sir Nicholas — but perhaps I had
better not present him . . . under the circumstances . . ."

"No, Iford, I do not suffer beasts . . . except on four legs. As for yourself, if you have a
spark of manhood remaining, help me to conduct this poor fuddled girl to her distracted
mother."

Without a word, Viscount Iford crossed the
room and, striking away Sir Nicholas Frayne's
detaining hand, set his arm about the now-
weeping girl and led her downstairs to the wild
embrace of her frantic mother who, having her
child safe in her bosom, slapped, kissed and
hurried her away, pouring benedictions upon
the head of 'her good, kind, brave ladyship.'

"Umph-humph!" quoth Miss Janet, placing
the broken bottle neck carefully on the mantel-
shelf out of harm's way and stabbing upward

with long forefinger, "The Gaddarene swine were no' sic loathly beasties as yon!"

"And you, Iford!" demanded my lady. "Pray, what have you to say?"

"Firstly, madam, that I heartily agree with Miss Janet that there are worse creatures than swine, and secondly to assure you that the girl, poor little fool, had only her own vanity to thank, and that she was in no real danger; you see, I was not asleep and — "

"You?" exclaimed my lady with look and tone of such blasting contempt that his pale cheeks flushed with a slow and painful colour. "Iford, it disgusts me now to remember that I used to kiss away your childish tears, cherish your boyish hurts and sorrows . . . oh, it is hard to believe you can possibly be the adored son of your sweet, gentle mother."

Viscount Iford turned to stare out of the window and with his face thus averted, answered very softly but in tone of such murderous hate that both ladies eyed him appalled.

"Remember, madam, I also had and have — a father! He is my excuse for what I am and may become. Had my sweet mother only lived

or . . . had he but died too, it is just possible
I might now be more worthy her love . . . yes,
despite him, it is just possible. . . . Ah — my
father! This right noble Earl! This so gallant
gentleman that . . . killed her . . . inch by
inch . . . hour by hour! When I think of my
mother, so gentle, so helpless . . . and all he
made her suffer . . . the bitter tears, her long
agony . . . I marvel how and why I have not
killed him, — as I may yet — "

"Iford — oh, hush! He is your father!"

"Madam, I prefer to know him as — the
noble Earl. To strike him dead would, I think,
be an act of filial piety to my loved mother's
sweet memory."

Here he turned and, beholding their looks
of horror, laughed a little wildly and striding
to the door, flung it wide, then bowed to them,
hand on heart.

"Ladies," said he with a flourish, "I have
the honour to wish you good-bye and a pleasant
journey."

But in the act of departure he paused and
looking on their faces, once so kindly familiar,
he spoke with warm, youthful impulse:

"Dear Lady Vibart and you, Miss Janet, whatever the dark future may hold for me, I would beg you both to believe that I love that small, gentle saint, my mother, as much, or more, in death as in life . . . and remembering this, I would have you think of me as kindly as you can — whatever be the end of me. Good-bye — "

"Wait!" said Charmian, her rich tones suddenly very gentle. "Where are you going, Iford?"

"Most possibly to the devil," he answered, lips curled in their cynical smile, "treading dutifully in the steps of my sire, the noble Earl . . . force of heredity . . . no influence strong enough to restrain me or counteract my — parental curse."

"Suppose I ask you to go with me to Cambourne — to stay a while — what would you say, Valentine?"

"Ah, my lady, when you name me so and look at me so sweetly kind, — almost like my own mother, — I would die for you!" He said it with such breathless eagerness and his eyes aglow with such light that she could not but believe him and, so believing, reached him her hand.

"Oh, Valentine," she murmured, "I could love you again for your sweet mother's sake and might do for your own. Come with Janet and me to Cambourne."

The young Viscount looked down at this shapely white hand lying between his own, then stooped yellow head, kissing it very fervently.

"Such tender friendship will be my comfort," he murmured, "and you so dear that I will not trouble you with myself, dogged as I am by such parental curse — "

"Ah, wilful boy," she exclaimed, "you exaggerate, of course, and must go your own way. But for the old days of innocence when you and my Richard were happy children together, and because of what might still be, I pray God keep you ever in His loving care, Valentine."

"Madam . . ." he breathed, "oh, my lady." Then, cynicism and dignity alike forgotten, he stumbled blindly from the room, closing the door behind him.

"Aweel," quoth Miss Janet, "the puir laddie was a wee fou', o' course, wi' sic wild galli-

maufry o' killing and death . . . and his ain
father! Hoot-toot, 'twas fair awfu'! And yet,
m' dearie, he looks verra young, verra delicate
and no' sae muckle changed frae the sonsy wee
bairn we kenned him yince. 'Tis sad, bitter
young soul, yon!"

"And dangerous too, I think, Janet, — dangerous and far, oh far, more deadly than his
wicked father."

CHAPTER IV

Tells how and why Sir Peter Started on a Journey

IT was evening when Sir Peter reached home to be greeted by Mr. Mordaunt (eyes more ox-like than ever) with the news of his lady's sudden departure. Mutely he nodded and coming into his library, found Charmian's note set conspicuous on his desk.

With hands not quite so steady as usual he broke the seal and read the message hastily, read it a second time with more deliberation and sinking wearily into his chair, became lost in a profound and gloomy reflection.

He had sat thus some while, staring blindly at the open letter before him, when he became aware of a familiar tramping thump, of knuckles on the door that opened and into the room stumped a tall man, very neat as to dress and upright of bearing, albeit he had only one leg.

"Axing pardon, Sir Peter!" said he, coming

to abrupt halt, "but, sir, me knocking and you not giving no answer, I naturally thought as the libree was empty, sir. I come to bring ee a foo flowers, Sir Peter; picked 'em for ee myself, I did — leastways, that is to say, Susan and me did."

"Come in, Tom! Come in and sit down."

"Thankee, sir. But these here flowers — ?"

"Lay them on the desk. Now sit down. I . . . want to talk to you."

"At your service and all attention as ever, sir!" said Tom, and forthwith sat down, his wooden leg levelled straight before him rather like a gun aimed at an invisible foeman.

"We've known each other a number of years now, Tom."

"Nineteen come the seventh, sir. Ah, ever since my hoss dropped dead atop o' Pemb'ry Hill and my carrier's business was ruinated in consequence."

"You have watched my son grow to manhood, Tom."

"Ay, sir, and a mighty fine young gentleman Mr. Richard be! Lord, wot a nofficer he'd 'a' made!"

"Have you ever seen me . . . harsh with him?"

"Never, sir, — leastways only when needed and all correct, — me, like yourself, sir, being strong for discipline."

"Hum!" quoth Sir Peter. "What do you mean exactly by discipline, Tom?"

"Law norder, sir! Obedience! Keeping a strong hand when and where needed and all rankings in their doo and proper place."

"Would you say I was a — strict father, then?"

"Why, no, Sir Peter, no — not wot you might hardly go for to name 'strict', no! A bit stern-like, p'raps."

"The strong, high hand, eh?" murmured Sir Peter. "Tom, you mean that I am a . . . strong father?"

"Ah, as iron, sir! As steel, Sir Peter — "

"And consequently, Tom, not . . . weak enough to stoop and make a friend of my son . . . to be his companion as well as his father, — eh, Tom?"

"No, sir! Not you! That aren't your sort, no, no! No more than the commanding officer can go amaking friends wi' rankers. Lord, no, it can't nohow be done — it aren't done, or well, — wot o' discipline, sir?"

"What indeed, Tom! Though to be sure I am not an officer nor is — " Sir Peter turned almost eagerly at a soft rapping on the door and rising with the same unwonted eagerness, frowned as Mr. Mordaunt appeared instead of a certain other so-yearned-for presence.

"Well, Mordaunt?"

"The Earl of Abbeymere, sir! He is outside, sir, on his horse; he desires a word with you, Sir Peter."

"Then ask his lordship to trouble himself to dismount and have the goodness to step this far."

"And . . . these here flowers, sir?" enquired Tom, rising hurriedly. "P'raps I'd better — "

"Leave them here, Tom, and thank you for the thought of them."

" 'Twas my pleasure, sir," answered Tom and, saluting with old-soldierly smartness, he stumped away. . . .

Ponderous tread of feet very deliberate and

loudly masterful . . . and the wide doorway
was blocked and filled by a presence; for my
lord the Earl of Abbeymere was very large in
everything corporeal except his eyes, which
were remarkably small and bright as glass;
also, like his footsteps, he was deliberate, masterful and loud with a seeming jocosity.

"How do, Vibart, how de do!" quoth he, advancing with heavy tread and large gesture of
heartiness. "Ya charming spouse is well, I
hope. God bless her warm loveliness! Ya Lady
Charmian is blooming as ever, hey?"

"Thank you, Abbeymere — "

"And young Richard, ya hopeful Dick? Sinning in all health and vigour, I trust? Pooh,
man! Don't look down ya nose at me! Youth
and health and sin go together, — always did
and always will! And your son's no better than
any other hot-blooded gentlemanly young
scamp, devil a bit, — my own lad, f'rin-
stance — "

"A chair, Abbeymere?"

"Thankee!" said the Earl, seating his bulk
in an adjacent armchair. "But talking o' my
own scamp — where is the cub? Ha' ya seen

him slinking anywhere hereabouts, neighbour?"

"If you allude to Viscount Iford — "

"Oh, Gad, Vibart, ya know I do!"

"Then Abbeymere, you should be aware that since his difference with my son Richard at Oxford, he has ceased visiting Holm Dene."

"Ha, these young bloods! They fell out, aha, quarrelled over some pretty trollop, I wager?"

"You received my letter, Abbeymere?"

"My dear fellow . . . did I?"

"Concerning my improvements at Fitworth."

"Improvements? My very dear fellow! At Fitworth?"

"My lord, you are perfectly informed of them, as I know."

"No, but am I? Improvements, says you! Egad, I've heard something about widening some lane or other thereabouts, Vibart, and cutting down some of my trees, — oh, yes. But as for — improvements, — "

"I am draining an unhealthy swamp, Abbeymere, and making an almost impassable lane into a road. That marsh has been the direct cause of much sickness in the village; the lane too is almost a morass in the wet weather."

"Ah, my dear good Vibart, you are so damnably, so very uncomfortably full of good works, but — what about cutting down my noble trees, hey?"

"There are but three to be felled, as I duly informed you in my letter of the twelfth instant — "

"But, Sir Peter, my own dearest, best of fellows, I have a peculiar passion for all trees, especially mine own . . . shady things, Vibart, picturesque and so on."

"By permitting my people to fell your three trees, Abbeymere, and running my road across that long-contested right of way, you may save me some hundreds of pounds — "

"But then, Vibart, you are so infernally opulent, so confoundedly wealthy, and my trees . . . I love 'em, my dear fellow, every one, root and branch, leaf and twig — "

"My lord, you need say no more. The road shall take another direction. It was for this neighbourly kindness that you honoured me here, I think?"

"Not altogether, Vibart, no. I rode over primarily in the interests of our class, to venture a faint, a very humble remonstrance of your persistent tenderness for malefactors, — rogues, vagrants and — poachers, dammem! Your too mild mildness as a magistrate and justice — "

"As to which," retorted Sir Peter, his dark eyes glittering, "your comments will be useless as unwelcome, my lord."

"But Vibart, my very dearest fellow, your methods are surely a direct encouragement to — "

"My lord, I suggest we talk of other matters," said Sir Peter gently, though with such look that my lord, lounging back in his chair, laughed but — was dumb; and laughing thus, his eyes seemed, in the large expanse of his comely face, more remarkably small and glassy than ever.

"Why then," quoth he, smiling into Sir Peter's sombre face, "what better subject than her ladyship — ya glorious Charmian? Pray suffer that I ha' the joy to see and pay her my humble respects, — now tush, my good Vibart! Why look so curst puritanical and austere? Re-

member I knew and adored her long before
you, — we all did, ha — from the Prince Re-
gent down! See now, there was myself and
Slade and Sherry and — ha, b'gad — Willoughby-Gafton and Alvanley, — not forgetting the famous Buck, ya cousin Maurice. We
were all her devoted slaves, and no wonder.
But the wildest, maddest, most determined of
us all were young Willoughby-Gafton and
Maurice! They yearned for each other's blood,
my dear fellow, three times on the point of
shooting each other . . . only prevented by
Prinny. Aha, we knew how to love in those days
— blood, fire and passion! And she was worth
it — beauty such as hers is always a joyous tan-
talization to live or die for — especially to such
as have made charms feminine their hobby, as
we did — and none more so than ya very humble servant."

"And now," said Sir Peter, rising all graceful ease and reaching for the bell rope, "now,
my lord, will you take a glass of sherry before
you go?"

The Earl stared up into the impassive face
above him, chuckled, leaned back in his chair

and laughed so very heartily that his eyes
seemed to vanish altogether.

"Oho, Vibart!" he gasped. "What a dear,
quaint, amusing fellow you are! And let it be
port, neighbour, port!"

Long after the Earl had departed, Sir Peter
sat frowning at his wife's letter in unhappy
meditation; at last he rang for a horse to be
saddled, but when Mr. Mordaunt appeared to
inform him the animal was at the door, Sir
Peter ordered it back to the stable with look
and tone of such sudden and unwonted peevish-
ness that Mr. Mordaunt's hatchet face seemed
all eyes.

Mr. Mayhew, the grey-haired butler, knocking tenderly, appeared softly to announce that
dinner awaited, and was distressed and not a
little shocked to learn, in words succinct and
peremptory, that his dear master would not
dine.

Entered thereafter, with propitiatory cough
and rustle of black silk gown, Mrs. Mayhew
the housekeeper, murmurously solicitous.

"A wing, Sir Peter, and a merrythought!"
she cooed, placing a daintily filled tray before

him. "Cut by my own two hands for ee, sir!
And a glass sir, of your favorite sherry . . .
Come now — do!"

Sir Peter frowned, smiled, sighed and —
did. That is to say, he was half through an utterly tasteless meal when down went knife and
fork and up he started, for his quick ears had
caught the yearned-for sound of horse-hoofs
beyond the open window. 'His Charmian had
returned to him — thank God!'

So forth he sped to meet and welcome her
. . . then paused to stare, chilled with sense of
loss, bitter disappointment and sudden apprehension, for riding towards him through the
fragrant dusk was a stranger on a foam-spattered horse, a very dusty man who, touching
dusty hat, drew rein.

"Sir Peter Vibart?" he enquired, opening
the wallet he bore.

"I am he."

"This letter, sir. Express from Paris."

"Ah . . . from Paris?" Taking the letter,
Sir Peter broke the seal and scanned its con-
tents hastily in the failing light.

"Will there be an answer, sir?"

"No. I will send my servants for your horse
. . . and your refreshment."

Seated again in his library, Sir Peter read
through the letter once more, his brows dark
with trouble and a keen anxiety, — these words
scrawled in desperate haste and very evident
agitation.

My dear Sir Peter,

It is in the utmost distress and perturbation
of mind that I write (unknown to Richard)
imploring your instant presence here in Paris,
your son Richard having involved himself,
(how, I do not justly apprehend) in a quarrel
with one who scraped acquaintance with us
some time ago, an elegant, very gentlemanly-
seeming person (though of years older, I suspect, than would appear) originating in some
trifle, the exact nature of which is (to me) yet
a mystery. But alas, Sir! my horror and despair
will be instantly manifest to you when I pen
the dreadful fact that a meeting has been demanded by the offended gentleman, accepted
by Richard and the awful result will be a duel.
This dreadful affair is arranged for the twenty-
fourth inst. six days hence. Your unfortunate
son goes out to be shot by a person twice his age
and (I gather) one who is accounted a very
deadly and most experienced duellist and man

slayer. In these tragic and most unhappy circumstances haste, haste, I implore you, to the aid of your desperate (and perhaps doomed) son, and the relief of your agonizing, anxious yet faithful servant to command

Tobias Chantrey.

P.S. I indite this epistle in secret and against R's expressed wish and command.
P.P.S. The person's name appears to be Henry Willoughby-Gafton.

Sir Peter rang and ordered valises packed for a journey abroad; then, taking quill and paper, wrote this:

Dear Heart,

I have sat here hoping and awaiting your return. Instead comes this letter, which speaks eloquently for itself and is the occasion for my instant departure for Paris.

So I may not see you again soon as I had hoped. Yet here may be the opportunity to prove my fatherhood. For come what may, my Charmian, this duel shall be averted and Richard shall come safe back to you. As for myself — know that, despite all other seeming, I love you with all that I am, now in this life and in the beyond, and rest

ever your truly humble Peter
and loving husband.

"Mordaunt," said he, sealing this letter, "I'm for Dover and Paris. Order a horse, tell Adam I'll ride 'Wings' the sorrel and hurry, man!"

"Dover, sir? But the packet doesn't sail until past midday to-morrow — "

"No matter; I'll ride to-night. And — this letter — when I am gone, bear it to my lady at Cambourne. You should arrive in two hours or thereabouts, if you ride hard. I wish it delivered to-night, Charles."

"Her ladyship shall have it to-night without fail, sir."

Then Sir Peter arose and in this so orderly house was unwonted bustle to such purpose that very soon, cloaked, booted and spurred, he was astride his eager horse.

"I shall be at our usual inn," said he to Mr. Mordaunt, who stood at his stirrup, "the Soleil d'Or in the Rue Royale."

And thus, with a last very wistful look up and around at this ancient house, this home he had loved so much, Sir Peter lifted hand in farewell to the clustered figures of his servants in the lighted doorway and galloped off into the gathering darkness.

CHAPTER V

Tells how Charmian Leapt to Action

CHARMIAN, sitting before the newly kindled fire in her bedroom of this vast, seldom-occupied house of Cambourne Lacey, shivered and wailed:

"A hateful, damp barracks of a place, Janet!"

"Hoot-toot, ma dearie, dinna swear — "

"Nonsense! I said 'damp'! And if swearing could comfort me, I'd swear — hard!"

" 'Tis grieving y' are for your Peter, forbye — "

"Absurd!"

"If ye'd taken my advice, Charmian Sophia, ye'd be home the noo, — ay, and warrum in the comfort of his arrums! Aweel, to-morrow we can start back after breakfast and — "

"We shall not!"

"Then hoo lang maun we bide here like twa lane corbies in a — "

"This all depends on the man's own stubborn pride."

"Charmian, ye dinna mean . . . my dear, you never intend to wait here until he — "

"I do! I will not stir a yard until he comes to take me home."

"Home! 'Tis sweet word, Charmian! Ah, 'tis a worrud to greet upon! Home again, — back to his soft-footed servants, his persistent, pervading care! Greet, my bairn! Cry, Charmian, weep awa' your pride and to-morrow we'll gang back — "

"Oh, hush, Janet, and go to bed — ah, no, dear, stay and share mine, — this huge chamber gives me the horrors!"

"And yet 'tis no larger than your room at Holm Dene, though to be sure your husb — "

"Be silent, Janet!"

"Aweel, the puir man, I jalouse 'tis dree and waefu' he is at this moment — "

"Indeed, I hope so!" said Charmian, between white teeth.

"And what'll we dae here at Cambourne?"

"Visit my tenantry, every village, every cottage on the estate. Talk with my agents . . .

bailiffs, stewards. . . . pore over accounts that I sha'n't understand — hark! Goodness me! What's that?"

Charmian started up, gazing towards the curtained doorway, her eyes wide in sudden frightful expectancy; Miss Janet rose and took up her ponderous reticule; for the great house, above them and around, seemed to reëcho to a furious knocking.

"Who . . . what can it be?" gasped Charmian, crossing towards the door. "Janet . . . oh, my dear, I feel, I know something dreadful is waiting for me . . . out there in the windy darkness. Come, let us go and face it!"

So saying, she opened the door and with Miss Janet bearing lamp in one hand and large reticule in the other, came to the great, deep stairway. In the hall below a solitary candle flickered, voices spoke in rapid question and answer.

"Oh, Janet . . . my loved Peter! God forgive me, something has happened . . . that is Charles Mordaunt's voice!" Then with flutter of dainty draperies she was down the stair, to see John Marshall, her aged butler, bearing a candle and in its light the mud-spattered, wind-blown form of Mr. Mordaunt.

"Charles — ?" she whispered.

"This letter . . . ah, no, dear madam, there is no cause for such alarm."

Stooping to the candlelight, she read Sir Peter's letter and was dumb; she read the enclosure and uttered a long shuddering gasp; then looked from poor Mr. Chantrey's hysterical effusion to the three anxious faces with eyes of such tragic despair that Miss Janet cried out like one stricken:

"Charmian! Ah — what is it?"

"Death, Janet!" she whispered. "Death for my Peter . . . or Richard . . . unless — oh, read, read it!" And now, while Miss Janet scanned these fateful missives, she turned where stood young Mr. Mordaunt viewing her with great eyes of unutterable sympathy, and questioned him breathlessly of Sir Peter: How was he? What had he said? How did he look? What were his last words? Questions Mr. Mordaunt answered, fully as might be, while she hung upon his every word.

"And he rode that same hour? Ah, this was like him!"

"Yes, madam, just so soon as he had written to you . . . though the Dover packet does not sail until after midday to-morrow — "

"So much the better — for I shall sail to-night. So pray, Charles, rouse the stables, order fresh horses to the carriage."

"Oh, but dear madam, dear my lady, it is a bad night and threatens worse — "

"What matter? No weather shall stay me, pray God! Go, Charles . . . fresh horses, — hurry, hurry! And you, Marshall, wake Mrs. Mollison and the maids . . . bid them to me instantly; we must be packed and away in half an hour."

"Away is it?" enquired Miss Janet, as they sped back again upstairs. "Ye mean to Paris?"

"Of course," answered Charmian, pointing to a certain line of her husband's letter. "You see what he says here? Janet, he means to save Richard at all hazards, which means his own dear self . . . to risk his life for our son."

"To Paris!" repeated Miss Janet, as they bustled to and fro to haste their departure. "And what can we do in Paris, — two, lone, feeble women, — what?"

"Save them both, of course. I must, I will or

— die too! And you see, Janet, oh, you see who it is strikes at me, my very heart and soul, after all these years?"

"Ay — I saw!" answered Miss Janet in unwonted agitation. "Who would it be but . . . Henry! Your old playmate . . . Willoughby-Gafton. He swore vengeance on ye long ago . . . oh, Charmian, oh, my dear!"

"But — after all these years! And to strike at me through my son! . . . Henry was cruel as a boy, wicked as a youth and — is merciless as a man, it seems, — an evil creature always!"

"And loved you, Charmian!"

"A wild, destroying love, Janet!"

"Ay, 'twas a love that destroyed his own career; — ye'll mind how he challenged Maurice Vibart and Lord Alvanley and even dared affront Royalty and was dismissed . . . and a' on account o' yoursel', Charmian."

"And — planned his own uncle's death, Janet! You have that damning letter yet . . . thank God you kept it!"

"Ay, being an unco' canny body, ye ken, I hae yon letter at Holm Dene —"

"Then to Holm Dene we must go . . .

Dress, Janet, dress! . . . And then to Seaford — "

"Ah, ye never mean those smuggling
bodies?"

"Of course I do. You know how I have stood
between them and imprisonment . . . and
they are all my friends, the Nyes and Potters
. . . Well, they shall sail us to France this very
night. We are racing Peter to Paris."

"Race, is it? But he'll be afore us on the
road, — miles."

"But we'll be before him on the sea —
leagues — and first in Paris by hours, Janet,
hours!"

And now, very full of anxious questions,
came the housekeeper Mrs. Mollison with her
two maids to fold and repack dainty dresses,
frills and furbelows, and all so speedily that
Charmian was tying the strings of her coquettish bonnet when Mr. Mordaunt came to inform them the carriage was ready and to plead,
with eloquent lips and soulful eyes, the privilege of escorting them.

Then downstairs they went out into a windy
darkness where the carriage stood, its lanterns

gleaming upon sleek horses that snorted and pawed eager hoofs, impatient for the road.

"Oh, listen to that moaning wind!" said Charmian, glancing round about and up at the sky, where a fitful moon peeped through flying cloud-wrack. "My poor Janet, I fear it is going to blow! John!" she called up to the dim-seen coachman, "To Holm Dene and drive fast, John, fast!" Then she ascended nimbly into the vehicle, followed by Mr. Mordaunt, and they were whirled away.

"Blow, is it?" moaned Miss Janet. "Why then, if oor ship isna' wreckit, 'tis mysel' will be — wae's me!"

CHAPTER VI

TELLS HOW CHARMIAN WENT TO SEA

HOOFS thundered, wheels rumbled, the carriage rocked and swayed, but Charmian, leaning in corner of the speeding vehicle, seemed now entirely composed, from the little feather of her small bonnet that swept about the beauty of her face, to the slim feet that cuddled each other beneath the dainty hem of her robe; for her eyes were quick with lively purpose and brightly alert, her chin was firm set and resolute, — she was indeed her most tranquil, lovely and capable self.

"We can buy clothes in Paris, of course," said she suddenly, "but while we change horses at Holm Dene I think we should pack my blue poplin and a few extra pairs of shoes."

Jingle of harness, rumble of wheels, clatter of galloping hoofs . . . blood horses these that seemed to know nothing of weariness or fatigue until they had jingled, rumbled and clattered to their destination.

"Jest two hours, my lady, near as may be!" quoth the coachman John, as his mistress alighted.

"That is well!" she answered, nodding up at him in the glare of the carriage lamp. "Now change horses for Seaford; drive the grays, John, and don't spare them, — hurry, hurry!"

By this time doors had opened, lights beamed and the place was astir; and now ensued such a running to and fro, such bustle and to do as even this much experienced old house had seldom known. And thus in remarkably short time:

"Janet," sighed my lady, back in her corner of the speeding carriage, serene and composed as ever, "we should reach Paris at least thirty hours before Peter."

"Paris!" echoed Miss Janet grimly, her high-bridged nose combative, her grey eyes truculent. "Yon sinfu' ceety! And what then?"

"We must seek out Henry Willoughby-Gafton instantly!"

"Oh! And — what then?"

"We must be guided by . . . circumstances. You did not forget that old letter?"

"My certie, — no! And what's mair, I hae this for him — if needfu'!" Opening her reticule which, like herself, was of an extraordinary size, Miss Janet drew thence a handkerchief, a thimble, a bottle of smelling-salts, a needlecase, an orange, divers other oddments and, lastly and with no little difficulty, a smallish yet very serviceable pistol.

"Heavens above!" ejaculated Charmian, blenching a little. "My dear soul, whatever — "

"Paris!" quoth Miss Janet darkly, tapping the weapon with long forefinger. "I'm no juist trusting ony Frenchman, m' dear! Guillotines! Heids on pikes! And—Henry Gafton! Ye'll ken Janet McFarlane was aye a cautious body!" And back went pistol, orange, smelling-salts, etc., in their due order.

"But Janet, oh, my dear, physical force cannot avail us against such as he, — that cold, sneering, merciless wretch!"

"Wha kens?" quoth Miss Janet, folding placidly powerful hands upon her bulbous reticule. "Twenty odd years syne I droppit him in the lily pool, ye'll mind. 'Tis peety he didna droon;—the ways o' Providence are unco mysteerious, I'm thinkin'!"

"That would be about two days after he wrote the letter, Janet."

"Ay, aboot."

"What a terrific splash he made! And how he looked at you . . . with murder in his eyes!"

"And sma' wonder! He was vera wet. But 'tis mair than looks I'll dare for you, Charmian, if need be."

"God bless you, I know this, my Janet! You have been my dear, patient, devoted Janet nearly all my life — "

"Ay!" nodded Miss Janet. "From the day you took a poor, friendless, shy pupil-teacher to be your loved companion, — swept me from sordid drudgery to . . . fairyland, a home where I — "

"Bullied me shamefully, Janet! Scolded, rated and railed at me but stood between me and the dangers my own follies might have wrought. Ah, my dear, what a spoiled, hate-

fully headstrong, perfectly odious child I
was!"

"And why for no? And you sae young, wi'
too much money and nae folk tae care for
ye—"

"But I found you, Janet! And yet I drove
you from me once . . . because of Maurice
Vibart. You so hated him, and I . . . drove
you from me—"

"Yet took me back, Charmian—"

"Ah, no, no; I implored, pleaded, begged
you to come back to me and you . . . . oh, kiss
me, Janet!" Here they embraced. "What a
little fool I was in those days and how strange,
how wonderful that the wildest of all my es-
capades should have led me to Peter and happiness . . . given me Richard . . . and this,
oh, this present horror of anxiety. For Janet—
oh, Janet, if we fail, it will mean death for my
Peter . . . death! I know it! Well, I must not
fail! At any—or every hazard I will not
fail!"

"No!" said Miss Janet, clenching powerful
hands upon her reticule. "There's yourself,
Charmian. And God. And . . . . me!" After

this was silence awhile save for the thudding horse hoofs and rattle of wheels.

"The more I think of it," said Charmian suddenly, "the more certain I am that this trumped-up duel with Richard is a plot to draw Peter to his death or — me to Henry Gafton's vile will. Yes, this is Henry's cruel vengeance on me. He knows Peter will never permit this meeting but will interfere . . . fight in Richard's stead. He has waited, Janet, waited all these years and now . . . ! Well, if they fight — if Henry attempts to shoot at my Peter — it shall be through my body . . . I'll throw myself between them and dare him to fire — "

"And I believe he would, Charmian, yes, and call it an accident. The man's a devil, a cold-hearted, pitiless monster, if he's fulfilled his early promise."

"So I believe, my dear. But then, Janet, the most desperately wicked man is — only a man, thank God! And no man is a match for a desperate, determined woman."

"Two!" snorted Miss Janet ferociously.

"Why, of course, — there are the two of us

and one of these a wife and mother! Oh, heaven
be thanked for you, my Janet!" Here a sudden
violent kiss. "With you beside me and a
cause so just — failure is impossible; oh, it
must be!"

"It shall!" nodded Miss Janet. "Have you a
plan?"

"Dozens!" sighed Charmian. "But not one
to please me — yet. Of course, we must keep
Peter from the very remotest chance of encountering Henry Gafton."

"Ay, but — how? Peter is an unco determined man, ye ken and — "

"I know he is, drat it! But I am also quite as
determined as Peter, but far less scrupulous
than he, and ready to be quite unprincipled to
save his dear life."

"Ay! But will ye tell me —"

"I will, dear, so soon as I've decided. . . .
We must pit Henry Willoughby-Gafton
against his own evil self, demon check devil!
We must! I will contrive this in some way. Oh,
Janet, I am Peter's wife and so terrified for his
safety that I fear nothing under heaven! And
you — you are my own dear, faithful Janet, as

courageous, as utterly determined and resolute
as I! So here are two of us! And — both
women! Well, let Henry Willoughby-Gafton
beware!"

"Ay!" murmured Miss Janet, fondling her
reticule. "Beware is the worrud! And oh, my
puir heart alive, — wull ye hark tae yon howling wind!"

And so, while they comforted and encour-
aged each other thus, the hoofs pounded,
wheels rumbled and clattered, the carriage
rocked and swayed through a riotous darkness
until they reached a bleak coast road fringed
by the white surf of a tumbling sea, where they
pulled up at last before a small, desolate, dim-
seen building that loomed blacker than the
dark.

"Be this the place, m' lady?" enquired the
footman, as Charmian let down the window to
peer.

"Yes, I . . . think so. Yes, it must be.
Knock, Sam, knock very loudly and enquire for
Mr. Nye." Forthwith Sam rapped lustily and
knocked amain until, after some interval, a lattice opened and a demurely nightcapped head

appeared, together with something very like a bell-mouthed blunderbuss, and:

"Below there!" roared a voice. "What's amiss?"

"It aren't no miss," Sam roared back indignantly. " 'Tis Lady Vibart it be!"

"Eh? Vibart?" quoth the voice. "Why then stand by!"

Forthwith the nightcapped head vanished and in remarkably short time a light glimmered, the door opened and forth came a sturdy fellow bearing a lantern, himself fully dressed and shod in great sea boots.

"Vibart, hey?" he enquired, stepping forward as out from the carriage window came my lady's feathered bonnet.

"How are you, Mr. Nye?" she enquired sweetly. "And is the baby well?"

"Lord love ee, yes, m' leddy!" he answered cheerily.

"Pray, is your son Ben at home?"

"Why, no, ma'm. Ben be at sea, I rackon, or — leastways theerabouts — mebbe."

"Then is Mr. Potter here, — Cheslett Potter?"

"Well, my leddy, 'e is an' then again I might go for to say 'e ain't, do ee see. Potter being a willy-wipsy sort of a chap."

"Oh, please, dear Mr. Nye, — couldn't you let me have a word with him?"

"Why, ma'm, I . . . dunno, me not being prezackly sarten sure, do ee see now. And yet again, seeing as it be your sweet leddyship, well, I might, if so be 'tis what ee might call important."

"Ah, Mr. Nye, indeed it is very, very important!"

"Well now," quoth Mr. Nye, "seeing as you's yourself, ma'm, and I'm I, and Potter's Potter and us arl friends like and comfortable to 'the trade', I dunno but wot I might so con-trive. Though, 'twixt you an' me, ma'm, us be main busy this moment . . . tubs, ma'm! And they preventives none too fur off. Hows'ever!" So saying, Mr. Nye took off the seaman's bonnet that now had replaced his innocent-showing nightcap and therewith veiled his lantern, giving forth two flashes and a flare. . . . And lo, — presently, above moaning wind gusts, was to be heard a trampling of heavy boots upon the shingle, dim forms flittered near, nearer, growing upon the straining vision into some half-dozen men who rolled in their gait, muttering hoarsely.

"Is Cheslett Potter there?"

"Ar, m' lady, here be Potter, ma'm," a hoarse voice answered and forth of his companions stepped a tall, broad-shouldered fellow who, coming boldly into the light of the carriage lamps, showed a smiling good-natured visage adorned by neatly trimmed whiskers, twinkling eyes and a broad nose with a heavenward tilt. "Here be Potter, ma'm, and the lads ready and willing for to sarve ee now as ever, my lady."

"Then can you sail us over to Calais?"

"Eh, to France, is it?" quoth Mr. Potter, clapping hand to booted thigh. "Well now, dannel me but our luggers be arl away, my leddy! Ay, arl on 'em to sea by reason o' they preventives. But . . . there be Pierre Cortot might tak' ye, ma'm, — yonder lays his lugger hove short, the *Jolly Filly,* my leddy, — out yon!" And Mr. Potter stabbed hairy finger out beyond foaming surf to a pitch-black sea.

"Now if so be as you wunt mind for to cross wi' Pierre — ?"

"Yes, yes!" cried Charmian, stepping down from the carriage with Mr. Potter's two big hands to aid her. "Of course . . . I will sail with any one so long as we reach France to-night."

"Why, Pierre be bound for Boolong, ma'm."

"That will do. But I don't see his boat; where is it?"

"My leddy, I'll show ee. Sim, pass the light."

Taking the lantern, Mr. Potter covered it with the skirt of his coat and therewith sent forth certain flares and flashes. "Now watch, ma'm, — over yonder!" And presently from that black and vasty ocean came answering flashes.

"Pierre be coming ashore, ma'm, and you'll find him a right trusty lad and good seaman although only a Frenchee, pore felly! But as I do tell him 'e can't nowise help not being born a fair an' free Johnny Bull."

"Yon sea sounds vera rough, Potterman!" wailed Miss Janet.

"Well, only a bit lumpish like, Miss Janet,

ma'm. Now lookee, if ee'll only try a pint of ale.warm, ma'm, and stirred wi' a sprig o' rue, you'll find it settle and lay on your stummick very sweet an' soothin', Miss Janet ma'm — "

"Horrors!" snorted Miss Janet, then caught her breath as through the white surf shot a small boat propelled by four thrashing oars . . . then a plump, smiling, comely fellow with rings in his ears stood before them who, finding these ladies could speak him in his own tongue, laughed for sheer joy and uncovering curly black head, bowed them into his boat with the grace and courtesy of any grand seigneur.

Miss Janet moaned distrustfully, shuddered violently but stepped into the rocking boat like the truly valiant soul she was.

And thus at two o'clock (or thereabouts) of a dismal, squally morning, Charmian, Lady Vibart, was rowed aboard the French smuggling lugger *La Jolie Fille* and set out, with her devoted companion, to risk and adventure all (even life itself) for those she loved so much and far beyond the telling.

CHAPTER VII

Introduces Three Fine Gentlemen and a Man

MR. HENRY WILLOUGHBY-GAFTON, having just done himself the honour of shaving himself, paused to survey the result in the very inadequate mirror, since it showed no more than his face, and this but dimly, — a nearly handsome face, pale, high-nosed, arrogant and adorned by glossy whiskers perfumed and curled in the latest mode, a chin deeply cleft and heavy red lips that, parting, showed two rows of very white, very perfect and exceedingly sharp-looking teeth.

Having bestowed an anxious scrutiny to the dark, thick curling locks at his temples and culled thence a too obtrusive white hair, having lavished profound and elaborate attention upon a spot on his almost too prominent chin, Mr. Willoughby-Gafton sat down to his breakfast; which Spartan meal duly disposed of, he transferred his languid person to an armchair and took up the morning *Gazette*. The armchair, like the apartment, was dingy and somewhat comfortless, but Mr. Gafton's dressing gown, like himself, was a thing of splendour and he lolled with a gracious ease.

Suddenly however he stirred pettishly and scowled up at the dingy ceiling, whence came the sound of a small, sweet childish voice crooning a song.

Mr. Gafton pished and cursed and clutching the frayed bell rope in white, be-ringed hand, tugged violently. And after some while in answer to this furious summons appeared a short, placid, fiercely moustached man in a worn and faded livery; a squat, broad-shouldered, very powerful man.

"Ha, species of rat!" cried Mr. Gafton in glib French, "Malediction, — name of a dog, will you silence your howling brat!"

"Sir," answered the man in English, "she ain't mine and no more she ain't no brat, your honour. Shall I clear these here things?"

"But name of a name, fool, you've given her a home in defiance to my orders, practically adopted her."

"Seein' as her ma's dead and she ain't got no father, I 'ave, sir — "

"Well, oblige me by stopping that infernal squealing or — "

"Your honour, that ain't squealing; she's singin' to her dolly, sir."

"Dolly?" ejaculated Mr. Gafton feebly. "Death of my life!" And sinking back, he fanned himself with the news sheet.

"Shall I clear away these 'ere breakfast things, sir?"

"Robinet," murmured Mr. Gafton, still drooping, "you have not inherited or acquired sudden wealth?"

"Not as I knows on, sir."

"And God knows you get little enough out of me."

"God knows it!" repeated the other fervently.

"And yet, my poor ass, you saddle yourself with this little *gamin* — "

"As nobody, your honour, nor nothin', sir, ain't no'ow agoin' to part me from. And now shall I clear these — "

"Name of a devil — yes." So while man proceeded about the business, master surveyed him with a languid wonder and ever-growing disfavour.

"Robinet, my little cabbage," he murmured at last, "thou'rt a disgrace to me, a reproach, an eyesore, a constant reminder of Fortune's buffets; thy clothes, my cabbage, proclaim a poverty damnably genteel."

"Sir," answered the man, setting down laden tray with an indignant clatter, " 'tain't no fault o' mine. I've darned 'em 'ere and darned 'em there, I've patched 'em 'igh and patched 'em low — "

"Be silent, my rabbit, or be French."

" 'Tain't nowise possible, sir, me bein' Bob Medders and as Henglish as I sound. And wot's more, your honour, though I've growed these here Frenchee whiskers to your orders, 'tis agreed as I don't never 'ave to speak the French lingo 'cept afore company, 'twas agreed atwixt us years ago."

"I wonder," sighed Mr. Gafton plaintively, "now I wonder why I endure thee, my Robin?"

"Well, sir, I'm so precious cheap, for one thing — "

"And nasty, very, very nasty, my Rob."

"And, for another thing, your honour, there's reasons, — three on 'em, sir, and one is that theer young French lady as — "

"Robert!" exclaimed Mr. Gafton, forgetting to lounge, "I am amazed that you live; indeed, your continued existence and my own forbearance astonish me!"

"Well, sir," answered Bob, meeting his master's threatening look wholly unperturbed, "I'm pretty spry and, as I told you afore, having larned to write, I've wrote a letter which — if I was to be took off sudden-like, or give up to the law, or vanish away and not be heered of for — only a week, say — this here letter would be opened and read — which might prove a bit awk'ard-like for your honour."

"Ah, behold a cunning rascal, a rogue prevoyant!" murmured Mr. Gafton and yawned. "Well, well, my small cabbage, it seems we must live and let live, — a pity, but needs must."

"Sir, ever since you saved me from . . . you know what . . . I've served you faithful and well and, so long as you don't come it too 'ard

on me, well and faithful I'll serve your honour,
and nobody could say fairer."

"Then, my very bright soul, my faithful
gallows bird, oblige me by stepping round to
the gunsmith's and — "

"They'm here, sir."

"Then pray bring 'em."

From dingy corner Bob produced a flat, ob-
long oaken case which he set on the table before
his master and opened, disclosing a pair of
murderous-looking duelling pistols. Mr. Willoughby-Gafton examined them with the eye
of a connoisseur, levelled and snapped them
with a practised hand, nodded and shut them
away.

"Sure death at anything from fifteen to
thirty paces!" said he and yawned again.

"Another dooll, sir?" enquired Bob, setting
the pistol case back in the corner.

"Well, let us say the final settlement of an
account long overdue. And I always pay my
debts, Robinet — that is — some of them."

"If your honour could pay me a trifle on account — "

"I said 'some of them', my poor fool and —

ha, now who the devil!" exclaimed Mr. Gafton, for a cracked bell had jangled harshly in the small outer lobby. "See who it is, Robin, and admit none but known friends. *Dépêche-toi!*"

Away down the narrow stone stairs clattered Bob forthwith, and, after some delay, returned accompanied by a rhythmic jingling, and announced in very excellent French:

"Monsieur le Colonel Louis Santerre!"

Framed in the doorway appeared a tall man, gloved hands crossed on gold-mounted, tasselled cane, scowling loftily beneath the brim of a hat jauntily cocked, a vast, extremely ferocious-seeming gentleman, for his glaring eyes, hooked nose and bristling moustache, all were supremely fierce; indeed ferocity clothed him like a garment, from hat crown to thudding spurred heels.

Mr. Willoughby-Gafton, without troubling himself to rise, saluted this imposing personage with airy motion of white hand, whereupon the Colonel bowed, stalked jingling into the room and depositing hat and cane upon the table, seated himself with a certain fierce emphasis.

"You have breakfasted, Louis?"

"But certainly, my dear Henri."

"Then a *petit verre?*"

"With pleasure."

"Robinet, the cognac."

And now while the Colonel sipped his brandy, Mr. Gafton glanced languidly through the *Gazette;* quoth he at last:

"It would seem that Victor's hand is as sure as ever. I see here that his man died last night."

"But certainly, my dear friend! Our Victor's ball took him in the groin, precisely where our Victor intended, — a slow death and painful, for Victor truly detested the fellow."

"You were the Vicomte's second, it seems."

"I had that honour, as you know I usually do. Victor expects it of me. As we drove to the ground, 'Shall you kill the poor devil?' says I. 'Not at once,' answers my Victor; 'I shall put my bullet where he will have time to feel it and — think about it.'"

"How like him!" murmured Mr. Gafton, with gleam of sharp, white teeth. "A truly angelic soul, our Victor! This makes his fifth fatality in as many months, eh, Louis?"

"Sixth, my Henri, his sixth — and five of them English!"

"Precisely!" nodded Mr. Gafton. "My compatriots are fools with either weapon, as a rule."

"With yourself as the brilliant exception, my Henri! You fight, my dear friend, especially with *l'arm blanche* with an abandon so joyous it is a pleasure to see — oh, charming . . . and no man in Paris so deadly with the pistol, except perhaps our Victor."

"Why except the Vicomte?" yawned Mr. Gafton.

"Ah? Ah?" murmured the Colonel, glaring at the brandy in his glass. "You think then if it should ever come to a rupture . . . you — he — ?"

"No, no," smiled Mr. Gafton. "I leave such thoughts to you, Santerre, eh, my gallant Colonel? But Victor and I understand each other. Are not we three — one?"

"Oh, but most certainly!" nodded the Colonel. "But tell me, how speeds thine own affair, my dear friend? With the young Monsieur Vibart?"

"Perfectly, I believe. We shall know more when Victor arrives; he is acting for me, as I think you are aware, and is with the young gentleman now."

"But my Henri, I am wondering! Mr. Vibart is — so wealthy and a gambler so reckless, — I am curious to know why his blood can be more desirable than his gold."

Mr. Gafton, lolling back in his chair, smiled and touched red lip with vivid tongue.

"My friend," he answered dreamily, "young Mr. Vibart possesses a . . . mother!"

"Aha!" exclaimed the Colonel and, smiling also, contrived thus to seem more sinister than ever. "Then, of a certainty, she is beautiful — ha? And beauty explains all — " Here the bell jangled discordant summons. Bob clattered downstairs again and presently reappeared to announce:

"*Monsieur le Vicomte Victor de Villebois!*"

And then into the room tripped a slim, blond gentleman, a small, plump, yet daintily exquisite creature, from the perfumed locks that clustered on white brow to little, glittering, varnished boots; his pink and white face seemed aglow with youth, his china-blue eyes danced with a light and joyous innocence. He clapped the ferocious Colonel playfully on broad shoulder, he embraced Mr. Gafton tenderly, and perching himself lightly on the table between them, swung one elegant, chubby leg gracefully to and fro; and yet somehow, as he looked gaily from one to the other, his youthful bloom seemed a little too fresh, his glad-eyed innocence a little overpowering.

"*Oh, la — la!*" cried he. "This Monsieur Vibart — so young but of a spirit — superb! He agrees to everything — place, weapon, distance, — everything! *'Comme vous voulez, monsieur!'* he says. He bows! He smiles! He is a young gentleman of a serenity, my faith, — an aplomb *veritable!* But — ah, yes! He desires the meeting shall be soon! Immediately! To-day! This morning, for example, if possible! Eh, Henri? How say you, my old fellow; will you favour this young gentleman so engaging by shooting him at once?"

"No, Victor. The meeting will be five — nay, six days hence — "

"But, Henri, my old fellow, I am amazed!

Name of a pipe, you astonish me extremely!"

"However, I have my reasons, Victor."

"Oh, perfectly!" nodded the Vicomte. "But then, Henri, after all — why shoot this so rich young gentleman; why kill — how say you? — the duck who produces us the eggs of gold, my old fellow?"

"Ha — thunder! Victor's right!" cried the Colonel, with ferocious snort. "As I say — why cut off the source of supplies, Henri, my friend?"

"To kill him," sighed the Vicomte, rolling his eyes, "my faith, but it is like — bounding into the visage of Providence! Why kill him?"

"It depends," answered Mr. Gafton. "I am hoping through him perhaps to bring down bigger game."

"Ah — I perceive!" cried the Vicomte. "It is the father you aim at! You will shoot the so honoured sire?"

"This depends also, Victor."

"Upon — what — my old fellow?"

"Upon — his lady wife."

At this the Vicomte was so affected that he was forced to leap from the table and embrace Mr. Gafton more fervently than before.

"Charming! Charming!" he exclaimed in gurgling ecstasy. "Woman! Woman! The hope, the inspiration, the beginning and the end so divine of heroical man! And, she is beautiful, my Henri? She is of a grace, is it not?"

"She is beyond description, Victor! The years have but mellowed, time hath but glorified her! She is indeed Femininity Essential!"

"Aha, a type provocative — yes? *Oh, la, la* — and it is she then you aim at, my old one — eh?"

"Precisely!" nodded Mr. Gafton. "To see her . . . on her dimpled knees! And . . . perhaps . . . in my arms . . . !"

"Ventre saint Gris!" exclaimed the Colonel, twisting fierce moustache savagely. "And so . . . thus . . . she saves alive her husband and her son — ?"

"Certainly!" sighed Mr. Gafton.

"My dear friend," cried the Colonel, "but it is magnificent! My felicitations! And we three are one — the fortune of one is the fortune of all, so — after thyself, my Henri — us!"

Mr. Gafton, lolling back in his chair, folded and refolded the news sheet into a paper staff wherewith he now gestured at the Colonel.

"Vicomte," said he wearily, "my dear Victor — regard well this Santerre! There are times when I marvel how we stoop to associate with this species of cur-dog, considering his manners which, as we know, smack damnably of the *canaille* — "

"Ha . . . a thousand devils!" roared the Colonel.

"Ten thousand!" sighed Mr. Gafton, "And may they be attendant about your deathbed, Monsieur the Colonel — "

"Death of my life, Monsieur! Would you quarrel with me?"

"But certainly!" murmured Mr. Gafton. "I have thought you would appear much pleasanter dead," and speaking, he smote Colonel Santerre across the face with his paper baton.

The Colonel leapt from his chair, six feet of blazing, speechless ferocity, thus before he could find utterance Mr. Gafton got himself afoot and looking upon the raging Colonel, smiled.

"Louis Santerre," said he, buttoning silken robe about his shapeliness, "my man of straw, fellow of bombast and thing of wind, your heart is a bubble, — in fine, you are no fit companion for me, therefore I propose to rid myself — and the dear Victor, of such offence." The Colonel strove desperately for adequate retort but, meeting the baleful glitter of the speaker's eyes, reading the deadly menace of his sharp-toothed smile, recoiled — glaring, but speechless still.

"Robinet," said Mr. Gafton, summoning his ever-imperturbable Bob, "load my pistols, — or this person may prefer swords — bring them!"

But here up jumped the Vicomte, hands uplift and eyes rolling.

"Sacred name!" cried he. "Oh, my faith, but this is truly frightful. . . . This cannot be, shall not be — no! Henri, my dear old one — dog cannot, should not, must not eat dog — "

"Dear Victor, a man — myself for instance, may tread on a slug — "

"Nay, now — hush thee, my old fellow; dear Henri, I protest thou'rt too severe — oh, beyond doubt! And you, Louis — ah, pray remember that between gentlemen of the hearts truly gallant, — Woman, the ladies, being divinities, are forever excepted and exempt. . . . You owe our friend Henri an apology."

The Colonel coughed, cleared his throat fiercely, glared ferociously at Bob and, turning to his master, bowed.

"Since Victor so adjudicates," said he harshly, "pray believe that I meant no offence."

"Nobly said, my Louis!" cried the Vicomte joyously. "Shake hands, my heroes! . . . And now let us forth and cement good-fellowship in a bottle, is it not? My faith it is — yes."

And thus they presently sallied forth together, — three very elegant, very imposing, very dangerous gentlemen indeed.

CHAPTER VIII

Which Gives some Description of a Mother and Son

Young Richard Vibart sighed deeply, ruffled his dark locks rather wildly and glancing despairingly at the litter of torn and crumpled letter paper that strewed the table, hurled aside quill pen and leaned back in his chair with sound very like a groan.

"Chantrey, it's no use!" he exclaimed. "I can't do it, Toby, I simply cannot find words . . . you see she . . . she isn't like an ordinary woman."

"Eh? Eh?" murmured Mr. Chantrey, without looking up from the book that engrossed him. "Ah, Richard, my dear boy, with what dispassionate art our divine poet introduces the approaching dismal catastrophe, the fall and ruin of famous Troy town! Hear him:

"'*Est in conspectu insulæ nomen Tenedos* —'"

"Oh, deuce take Virgil!" cried Richard,

leaping to his feet and pacing restlessly about the sunny chamber. "Wake up, Chantrey! They killed old Priam ages ago, but I'm very much alive — at present! Yes, and trying to write to — my mother, to say 'Good-bye' to her as cheerily as possible. So shut your Virgil, old fellow, and try to concentrate on my own approaching catastrophe."

Mr. Chantrey, a small, pale gentleman, closed book on finger and blinking pale eyes at his charge, stroked pale hair and sighed:

"Eh? Catastrophe? Oh, my dear boy, you . . . you mean — ?"

"I mean," said Richard, frowning at that litter of unfinished letters again, "that, in all probability, I have just . . . three more days of . . . of life — "

"Dreadful!" gasped Mr. Chantrey and dropped his book. "But oh, Richard . . . perhaps . . . there must be some way out . . . some escape, — there must be, there shall be . . . you are too young to . . . die!" Here the door behind them opened very stealthily the merest fraction.

"Oh, I don't know," said Richard, glancing

at his face in the mirror and frowning to see it
so haggard. "I've lived a whole nineteen years
and I've been — wonderfully happy . . . so
happy that I ought not to complain, though I
should like to . . . go on living, of course!
And I'm not afraid, Toby . . . not exactly,
no — I don't think so. But this waiting is rather
. . . damnable! I would to God it were over
. . . one way or the other. Why must Gafton
keep me . . . dangling in suspense? I . . .
can't think of anything else . . . I have but to
close my eyes to see it all happen . . . the early
morning . . . dew on the grass . . . birds
singing all about us, and then — the puff of
smoke! And myself face down on the grass,
blind forever and forever deaf . . . my body
dead and my soul . . . where, I wonder? It
keeps me awake, Toby, at night. And now I
don't know how to write to my mother. These
days of waiting have been rather . . . terribly
ghastly, Toby."

"Terrible?" cried Mr. Chantrey, getting
jerkily to his feet and clenching nervous hands
in his pale hair. "Oh, my good, merciful God,
they have proved a very nightmare, a torment-

ing hell to me — when I have not been reading!"

"But then you're a great reader, Toby, —
morning, noon and night your beak is in some
book or other."

"Yes, yes, I am, thank God!" cried little Mr.
Chantrey wildly. "I should have run stark mad
else. I read because I dare not think of you,
Richard, and what may happen in . . . the
immediate future. Your honoured father
placed you in my care — mine! Your father is
paying me very generously, ridiculously so
. . . he was ever my good friend years ago at
Oxford, and now . . .! If you should be
killed, Dick . . . and in my charge, how shall
I ever dare face him? Good God! What shall
I ever say? Sir Peter can be so terrible . . .
and you are his only son! Heaven help me, how
shall I ever meet Sir Peter?"

"My poor old Toby! *Nil desperandum et
cætera!*" said Richard, setting long arm about
the little gentleman's twitching shoulders. "My
father, I'll admit, can be rather a Tartar occasionally, as well I know, by George — "

"Terrible! Terrible!" wailed Mr. Chantrey.

"But he is always just, and so, old fellow, he cannot, will not blame you since I . . . I alone am responsible. Remember, I brought it upon myself, Toby! I struck the fellow, as I would again, damn him, under like circumstances. So mine alone is the blame and I am quite ready to answer for it — as I must."

"But his grief, Richard, — think of his grief! And your dear mother will — break her heart — "

"Oh, damme, Tobyman, no more of that! Tell me of . . . of my father . . . when he was young . . . at Oxford. Was he always so devilish stately, so damnably dignified and cursedly unapproachably aloof in those days, Toby?"

"No, no, he was very popular . . . with some. He was much like you, Richard, in some ways, only a leetle steadier and far more studious, yet a remarkable athlete and boxer, quite a singularly good boxer I believe and yet, my boy, a great lover of books and — "

"Books!" exclaimed Richard. "Well, get back to yours, old fellow. Read, Toby, read as much as you will but — no writing! Not a

word, not a hint! No letters to my mother . . .
the folks at home, remember! They must not
know of this miserable business until it's over
and . . . done! That's why I've been trying to
write to them all the morning . . . I managed
it to my father pretty well, I think, but I can't
find words to tell my — mother. I had nine
shots at it — shots, egad! But I just can't find
words, Toby; you see she . . . was always so
much more than a — an ordinary mother! So
read away, old fellow, but not a line home,
mind — until after! Remember you promised,
swore — "

"Swore, Richard . . . did I?" quavered
Mr. Chantrey. "Surely not, nay I'm positive I
never passed my oath — "

"Eh?" gasped Richard, staring, "why . . .
what . . . you don't mean — ?" In an instant
he was across the room and had his strong,
young hands on his tutor's thin shoulders, rocking the little gentleman to and fro. "Sir . . .
sir . . . Mr. Chantrey," he cried, "Toby, for
God's sake, don't tell me you — have written."

"Why, of course, Richard!" said a smooth
soft voice, and the door, opening suddenly

wide, showed Charmian, Lady Vibart, who somehow contrived to appear as daintily unruffled, from small bonnet to slim, sandalled feet, as tranquilly vital, as lovely and altogether adequate as ever in her life. "I owe Mr. Chantrey my deepest gratitude —" Then Richard had her in his arms.

"Mother!" he gasped.

"Wilful boy!" she murmured, her hands caressing this head, this face and hair so like her own. And this was all for a while . . . an eloquent silence wherein little Mr. Chantrey crept softly from the room.

Presently, their arms still about each other, she drew him to the table.

"Nine!" she murmured, nodding at the crumpled letters, "and all for me!" Then taking up one at random, she smoothed it gently and read from it in the same tender voice: "'Ever beloved and honoured mother!' Oh, Richard, am I? Am I indeed so loved and honoured? Never flush, silly boy! But do you truly love and honour me so much, my Richard?"

"More," he answered fiercely, "far more than I can ever write — or say."

"Yes," she murmured, "being so very English — and almost a man, of course, you could never show me all your heart until Death had crept so near. But — ah, Richard, it is heavenly to know you love me so — so desperately! You do, don't you?"

"Beyond words!" he answered, clasping her faster and bowing his head to her ready shoulder.

"Then, to be sure, you will obey me in everything and — absolutely?"

"Yes, Mother, in everything — that is to say, in everything except — " he faltered and raised his head to look at her a little apprehensively.

"So, of course, you will tell me where I may find this man, this Mr. Willoughby-Gafton?"

"No!" said Richard, head aloft. "Forgive me, dear, but indeed I . . . cannot."

"Oh, then Mr. Chantrey shall — "

"But, Mother, this man, Mr. Gafton . . . he is so . . . such a . . . he is not worthy to meet you . . . he or his friends! You cannot possibly — "

"Thank you, dear Richard, but I can and

shall. I fear no man! And I knew Henry Willoughby-Gafton when he was a boy — less than your age, Rick."

"Yes, he told me he knew you; this was really how we became acquainted."

"Ah . . . indeed!" said Charmian, beginning to frown. "Well, this is how I'll stop this hateful business."

"But, Mother, it's quite too late for any interference; it is quite . . . oh, quite impossible — "

"Nothing is impossible to a mother, foolish boy — especially this one! So tell me his address."

"But how can you visit this man, — you, Mother, you?"

"Very easily, dear. I have no apprehensions. Besides — our Janet goes with me."

"Janet! Is she here?"

"Of course, and will be down so soon as she has selected our apartments. So, Richard dear, give me this man's address."

Poor, harassed Richard tramped across the room to scowl out of the window, tramped back to frown at a picture on the wall, sighed, muttered, met Charmian's tranquil glance and spoke in desperation.

"But, Mother, I . . . you . . . it would be most irregular — "

"My dear, so much the better!"

"They will think me afraid," he groaned; "scorn me for coward . . . a terrified child begged off by his mother — "

"No, Richard, they will be confronted by a wife interposing between a murderous villain and her husband. I am here to save your father."

"My . . . oh, my father? Oh, but surely — "

"Yes, Richard, the dear soul is speeding here as fast as possible but I, of course, sped faster, thank Heaven!"

"You mean he is coming to — "

"Take this duel on himself, yes, Richard. He means to save you at all hazards and I am here to save you both. So tell me Willoughby-Gafton's address!"

Richard protested, reproached, pleaded, groaned, — and told her, of course. And, having done so, fell instantly to deeps of gloom, talking of his honour and manhood — like the

high-spirited boy he was, while she watched
him with her wise, beautiful eyes.

"Dear Richard," said she when he had done,
"never think I would shield you at cost of your
honour. But God has given me two men to protect, — yes, dear, to protect from their own
blundering manliness. He sent me your noble
father, He gave me you, and my dear, your
lives are too precious to be thrown away,
spilled and wasted in a manner so very futile.
And so, because I am, by God's blessing, wife
and mother, so, by God's help, I will end this
foolish, wicked, hateful affair somehow some
way . . . the way — ! and do it far better, I
hope, than any man with his swords and pistols.
But, Richard — as you love and honour me,
you must promise from your soul that neither
you nor Mr. Chantrey will suffer your dear
father to know or suspect that I am in Paris —
swear me this, Richard!"

"I swear!" he whispered, awed by something
in her look. "But — oh, Mother," said he, between laugh and sob, "how wonderful you
are!"

CHAPTER IX

TELLS HOW MY LADY CHARMIAN PLOTTED AGAINST HER LORD

DESCENDING from the *fiacre,* with Miss Janet in close attendance and extremely alert, Charmian bade the driver wait and turned in beneath an ancient, gloomy arch that gave upon a dismal courtyard whose one-time grandeur had long since departed; beholding the which sinister prospect, Miss Janet clutched her large reticule more firmly and, scowling round about, emitted that remarkable exclamation only Scottish lips may truly utter:

"Umph-humph!"

"What is it, Janet?"

"Guillotines, m' dear! Heids on pikes! The Carmagnole and corpses, m' love! The place fair reeks o' them!"

"Indeed it is very dismal, Janet, not at all what I expected—"

"His sinfu' years hae not exactly prospered him, I'm thinkin'—save us a', wha's yon!"

quoth Miss Janet and halted suddenly, poised for action offensive as from somewhere close by came a thin wailing.

"Why, Janet — it's a child! Over there in the corner, and such a mite!" And next moment my lady was bending to a very small bundle of woe. "It's a little girl," said she, and then in French:

"My poor little one, why do you cry?" The grievous bundle stirred, a very small, pale, elfin face bedewed with tears was lifted and a soft voice, sobs bravely stifled, made answer:

"Oh, Madame, I fell down and — behold, I bleed!" Here a little knee was exhibited raw from a recent mishap.

"Poor little bird!" murmured Charmian and gathering the child in her arms, she sat down on an old stone bench, a battered relic of past grandeur, and there, having wiped these childish tears and kissed this little, too pale face, she deftly bandaged this small knee with her dainty, perfumed handkerchief; then giving the child a comforting squeeze, she set her down and into the little hand pressed a bright, new silver coin, whereupon Miss Janet, diving

into her capacious reticule, produced the orange and thrust it into the child's other hand.
Thus enriched, the little creature stared from
one grand lady to the other, curtseyed demurely and, with sudden wistful smile, turned
and incontinent sped away on light, elfin
feet.

"Number seven, *bis!*" said Charmian, rising
and smoothing her voluminous skirts.

"Ay!" nodded Miss Janet, closing her bulky
reticule. "And the sooner we're awa' the better,
m' dear."

"Janet, is my bonnet straight, my hair in order?"

"Ay! But why trouble? — The man's a villain!"

"Truly, but then the villain is a man, my
dear!"

"Whisht!" cried Miss Janet, becoming
grimly alert as upon the quiet rose a hoarse
rumble of voices and into that quiet courtyard
came three men, rough-clad, desperate-look-
ing fellows, one of whom was short, grizzled
and very fiercely moustachioed. At sight of the
ladies, they hushed their talk and, standing in

remote corner, muttered together a while ere they separated.

"Number seven, *bis,* must be on the other side," said Charmian; "let us try." So came they at last to the number sought where yawned a doorway that led into a small lobby, and here in remote and grimy corner hung a rusty bell pull which my lady tugged firmly, whereat Miss Janet started and slipped two fingers into reticule as, high above them, a bell jangled harshly.

"I'm going up wi' ye, Charmian!"

"Certainly, dear. Though, of course, I must see him alone."

"Alone? But —"

"Hush!"

Heavy boots upon the stair in clattering descent and four very observant feminine eyes beheld a short, grim, fiercely moustachioed man, at sight of whom Miss Janet's hand vanished into the reticule altogether, and to whom Charmian addressed herself in fluent French.

"Don't talk it, lady," said he, with weary gesture. "You don't 'ave to. Me name's Bob Medders and I'm as Henglish as you be, I am — so don't!"

"Oh?" said Charmian, with look and tone of sudden friendliness. "Well, Mr. Meadows, I wish to see a Mr. Willoughby-Gafton — "

"Can't be, ma'm! Me master's out and won't be 'ome till Lord knows when."

"Ah!" murmured Charmian and thrust a coin into his unready hand.

"Eh, man?" he enquired, staring from the money to her bewitching face, just now smiling on him very kindly. "Wot's this here for, lady?"

"I wish to speak with Mr. Willoughby-Gafton . . . please . . . at once!"

"Why then, ma'm, all the gold in the mint aren't no good, — for ye see I'm tellin' ye gospel-true . . . me master's out."

Charmian's vivid lips pouted ruefully and her deep eyes held Mr. Meadows with a look kinder than ever.

"I wonder if you would permit us to see his apartments?" she murmured. "Just a peep!"

"Why, lady, I dunno! He don't never allow nobody 'cept his own pals and sometimes a . . . leastways not ladies — "

Charmian laid one shapely, gloved hand on his worn sleeve.

"Just one peep?" she murmured. . . . Bob Meadows fumbled with his fierce moustache undecidedly, then his grim features softened and touching finger to shaggy eyebrow, he led the way upstairs.

" 'Tain't wot you might call a pallis, ma'm," said he, opening the inner door, "no, it hain't no marble 'all and yet to-day it don't seem so bad, some'ow!" For Charmian had entered, filling that dingy room with her vivid, radiant presence.

"Not many books!" said she, glancing round about.

"And them only French!" quoth Bob. "But why books, ma'm?"

"To be sure! I am used to seeing books, — a great many!" she answered, her eyes suddenly wistful and tender. . . . So you are an English-man, Mr. Meadows?"

"Born in Sussex, I were, lady . . . but . . .

I went to London and ah, well, there be no
place like Sussex!"

"I live there, too, in the summer."

"Do ye, lady, do ye now! Lord, wot wouldn't
I give — if I 'ad it, — for a sniff o' the air and
a glimp o' the Downs 'long over Westdean
way! . . . But Sussex ain't for me — never no
more!" Now at this moment a door in remote
corner opened and a little elfin face peeped in
at them shyly, at sight of which Bob's naturally
harsh features were transfigured by a look of
such doting love that my lady, acting on swift
impulse, reached out her hand to the child.

"Come hither, little one!" said she in French,
whereat the child, timid no longer, fled to her
and cuddled down at her knee.

"Love me eyes!" exclaimed Bob. "Wot, lady,
and was it you as comforted of her down in the
yard, was it you, ma'm?"

"Yes," answered my lady, smoothing the
child's dark curls; "is she yours?"

"Well, ma'm, y' see her pore ma died and
she ain't got no pa so — I've took her over, as
y' might say."

"What is her name?"

"Well, ma'm, bein' only French, it's Nanette, but I calls her Nan. I'm a-teaching of her to talk proper English and a oncommon rapid larner she be."

"A sweet, lovable little soul, Mr. Meadows!"

"Ah, ma'm, she's all o' that."

"But she is much too pale!"

"She is, lady, though I feeds her reg'lar and the best I can or knows 'ow, but it don't seem to do no good."

"You love her very much, I think, Mr. Meadows."

"Ah, — you may say so, ma'm!"

"Then why don't you keep her alive?"

"Keep her alive?" gasped Bob in horrified dismay.

"Yes. She needs pure air and sunshine."

"Don't I know it, ma'm?" cried he bitterly.

"Well, why don't you take her away into the country?"

"Lord love you, lady — 'ow can I? Ain't I a slave and worse, and never no money — "

"Then why not earn money and be free? Why not earn enough to take her back with you to England — and Sussex?"

"Because this here ain't no age of miracles, ma'am!"

"Oh, yes, indeed!" said my lady placidly and still smoothing little Nanette's glossy hair. "Miracles happen every day only we don't recognise them as such. This miracle is that you may help me and be paid a great deal of money."

"Oh, ma'm? 'Ow much?"

"Two thousand louis!"

"Two thou — but lady . . . oh, lady, wot for . . . I asks ye?"

"For kidnapping a friend of mine."

"Eh . . . wot, ma'm . . . kidnapping . . . ! But why pick me for sich a job?"

"You look capable, and I saw you with two men in the courtyard who also looked — capable."

"And you want us to . . . kidnap . . . a friend o' yourn?"

"Yes, a . . . much loved friend. I should require you to take him out of Paris and keep him away for . . . three to six days. Ah, but — you would have to be very gentle kidnappers; wherever you take him he must find every comfort — if he were so much as bruised you would not have a franc — a centime."

"Sacred name! 'Tis a fortin' you offers, lady — if so be you ain't flamming — "

"Could you contrive it, Mr. Meadows?" she enquired, in the same placid tone.

"Lord, yes, my lady; the kidnappin's easy enough. I knows two or three coves as would be main glad o' the — "

"You would need at least four men."

"Why so, lady?"

"Because my friend is so very strong, so very brave and resolute."

"Well, I could get four — old pals as I can trust . . . if you ain't flammin' me . . . a joke, lady or — a trap?"

"Neither, Mr. Meadows; I'm desperately serious and to prove my good faith, come with me and I will give you five hundred francs as a pledge. Think of it, Mr. Meadows! Two thousand louis! A cottage in Sussex! And health and life for your little Nanette."

"Well — dash me eyes, lady — axing your pardon, ma'm, but this is a reg'lar go, this is — ah, rum ain't no word for it! But — always s'posin' as you ain't flamming — where is this gentleman and 'ow am I to know same?"

From the laces at her bosom my lady drew a miniature and gave it into Bob's hand.

"There he is, Mr. Meadows! He is tall and even stronger than he looks, so you will need to take him unawares . . . and be very, very careful, for if you hurt him —"

"No fear o' that, my lady; he'll be trussed up so cosy as I dunno what, afore e' knows it. Lord love ye, ma'm, this ain't the first time me and — wot I mean is, my lady, this here gent shall be sperritted away without s' much as rufflin' of his 'air — always supposin' as you ain't flammin' —"

"Come with me, Mr. Meadows, and the five hundred francs shall be paid you at once. And on the way I'll tell you when and where you may . . . take him — though without the least harm, mind!"

"Lady, 'e shall be handled gentle as any tender babe, I give ye my word and Bible oath on that! And now, if you'll kindly wait while I gives me face a sloosh —"

"Oh, Charmian! Oh, my dear!" whispered

Miss Janet in shaken voice, so soon as they were alone, "oh, but 'tis awfu' despret thing ye do — a wild, wild scheme!"

"Yes!" sighed Charmian, her dimpled chin rather more prominent than usual, "but desperate ills need desperate remedies . . . also, Janet, I believe in God!"

CHAPTER X

Concerning the Two Generations

FOAM-SPATTERED horses and a dusty chaise that racketed through billowing dust-clouds; and leaning from the open window a handsome, dusty gentleman whose aquiline features bore stern resolution in every line and who, loud above rattling wheels and hoof-beats, called for greater speed, backing his command with such proffers of golden bounty that the dusty postilion's dusty face grew resolute likewise.

Thus along far-flung highways bordered by innumerable trees, whirling through sleepy hamlets, clattering through the narrow streets of pleasant towns, rumbling over bridges, splashing through glimmering fords, this swaying, fast-travelling chaise bore Sir Peter Vibart on his hazardous venture.

Night was falling when he passed the barriers and nine o'clock striking as his chaise clattered into the courtyard of the inn of the Soleil d'Or, whereat was instant excited bustle and confusion; amid which hubbub two feminine heads, outthrust from window high above and wholly unnoticed, watched Sir Peter step forth of the dusty vehicle to be ushered indoors with many bows and flourishings of arms.

"The dear love!" murmured Charmian. "How splendidly English he looks! How masterful! How engagingly sinister! To think I must so mortify his dignity, or risk a hair of that loved, majestic head! And yet, Janet, if he be bruised indeed, as I fear he must be or . . . or even break a bone — which kind Heaven forbid — yet better so than suffer him to get himself shot! So creep away, Janet dear; go and warn the Meadows man — "

"Ah, must I, Charmian?"

"Instantly! Go — go before I grow foolish and weaken!"

Meanwhile Sir Peter having followed a deferential person upstairs to a certain door, dismissed him with a gesture and opening the door, beheld his son who, dropping the book he had been endeavoring to read, leapt from his chair and advanced in eager welcome.

"Father!" he cried. "Sir?" then paused, for Sir Peter's face showed pale and stern and his tall, lithe form seemed unapproachably stately.

"So," said Sir Peter, laying aside hat and riding whip, "you are become quite a man of the world, Richard!"

Now seeing the boy's shaken look, the quiver of his sensitive mouth, the slow, painful flush that swept from chin to brow, Sir Peter's severity relaxed and stepping forward, he laid both hands on Richard's drooping shoulders and gave him a little affectionate shake more eloquent than any words; then looking into his father's eyes, Richard smiled, though somewhat uncertainly and spoke from his very heart:

"Sir, . . . oh, Father, it's good . . . I'm glad to see you again. Are you here because . . . have you come to . . . second me — ?"

"No, Richard, no — to enquire into this unfortunate business and settle it — one way or another. Where is Mr. Chantrey, by the way?"

"He went to bed, sir, with a headache. But, sir, pray how do you propose to . . . to settle it — this affair?"

"That remains to be seen. However, I am sufficient of an egoist to believe that my . . . our son would not be involved in such affair without just cause."

"I thought it so, Father."

"Then be seated, Richard, and tell me all — or as much as you will."

"That will be all, sir. But first, have you dined?"

"No, indeed I'm not hungry —" But heedless of all protestations, Richard rang bells and so bestirred himself, (and others) that his father was very soon seated before a tempting meal. And now while Sir Peter ate and drank, his son, attending on him with filial solicitude, told his tale:

"I had remarked Mr. Willoughby-Gafton frequently as I rode in the Bois; he was always splendidly mounted, and at last we spoke . . . struck up an acquaintance. He seemed a very fine, dashing fellow, knew a great many people and was a member of several famous clubs. He introduced me to one or two where I . . . I gambled, sir."

"As you informed me in your letters, Rick."

"Yes, Father. But each night the stakes grew higher and — I generally lost."

"To him, of course!"

"Yes, sir, and to his friend the Vicomte de Villebois principally — "

"Yet it was not a vulgar quarrel over money, Richard?"

"No, sir, the cause was my — mother."

"Good Gad!" murmured Sir Peter, laying down his knife and fork. "The scoundrel!"

"No, Father, — it . . . it was not so much what he said but his manner . . . and in a gambling hell!"

"What were his words?"

"He congratulated me on possessing for mother a paragon of beauty and . . . chastity."

Sir Peter pushed away his plate and nodded gently.

"Well, Richard?" he enquired.

"He said, sir, that he had the felicity of her acquaintance upon a time."

"Anything more, Richard?"

"He said that . . . he and the bewitching Charmian, Sophia Sefton of Cambourne, had . . . had paddled together in the same brook."

"Yes, I believe they were children together . . . and what more, Richard?"

"Why then, Father . . . I hit him."

"Indeed, Dick?"

"Yes, Father, it . . . was something in his smile, his look, his tone . . . impossible to describe — however, I struck his smiling mouth . . . on impulse, sir."

"Hum!" murmured Sir Peter, but his eyes held such a look that young Richard caught his breath, and then was upon his feet for — his stately father was actually bowing to him and speaking in the same affectionate murmur: "Under which circumstances, Rick, I almost think my impulse would have been the same."

"Then, sir, you . . . you find no fault — "

"None, my dear Richard — ah — except those gaming hells! Once, yes, — twice, perhaps, — but thrice was merest folly! And yet I suppose a boy of nineteen — even your mother's and mine — must play the fool like the ordinary boys of other folks, though not so often, I trust — eh, Dick? And now I'll trouble you for Mr. Willoughby-Gafton's address."

"But Father — sir, pray what — ?"

"He lives in Paris, I suppose. You might give me the names of his clubs, also."

"Sir, pray . . . pray what do you intend?"

"Well, I shall — reason with him."

"But how, sir, how can you ever induce him to forgive that blow of mine?"

"By administering one or two of my own — if necessary."

"Ah, great God! Then you do . . . it is your intention to save me by forcing him to fight you, sir?"

"Always supposing there is no other way, Richard."

"Then, Father, I beg you, I entreat you to suffer me . . . for my own sake, Father — for yours, for my dear mother's — sir, I do implore you — !" Thus young Richard, his shaking hands outstretched, all passionate supplication from head to heel.

Sir Peter rose and taking those quivering hands in his own firm clasp, smiled and shook his head.

"Impossible!" he answered. "You see, Richard, my mind is quite made up."

"But Father," gasped Richard; "oh, my God . . . to think I have brought you . . . to this! They say he is sure death with either weapon, nobody to match him except perhaps the Vicomte — "

"A regular spadassin, Richard, eh?"

"Ah, sir, if — if he kill you . . . what of Mother?"

"She will have you, Rick!"

"It would kill her! Father, it would break her heart! And you are so young to — die."

"You are something younger, Rick. Yes, you are the new generation and it is quite right, quite natural and very proper that the old should pass on and give up — yes, cede everything to the new . . . but Lord, what foolish, sentimental to-do, boy! The meeting may never happen and if it should, I may come off unscathed. So do not distress yourself before the event. And now, Richard, favour me with Mr. Gafton's address and pray ring for a hackney coach, a *fiacre* or anything on wheels."

"May I go with you, Father?"

"Thank you, Dick, but this is an occasion when I would rather be alone."

"Then, sir, should it . . . come to a duel, may I have the . . . the honor of seconding you? Please, Father!"

"Gad, Richard, not for worlds! No, the Beverleys are in Paris, — Sir Peregrine will act for me, I'm sure — always supposing — hum! My hat and whip, pray . . . If the coach is not here, I'll find one, or walk." But at this moment came a waiter to say the carriage was below.

"I . . . I'll stay up until you return, Father."

"No, no, Richard — I have other calls to make and shall be late. . . . You're forgetting my whip!"

CHAPTER XI

BOB MEADOWS, clattering down the dingy stone stair, perceived by the aid of dim, uncertain light a tall, rather formidable, very autocratic gentleman who, surveying him with dark, piercing eyes, demanded instant speech with Mr. Henry Willoughby-Gafton.

"Wot name, sir?"

"No matter, — show me up."

"The master's engaged, sir — comp'ny, sir."

"No matter, — I'll go up." And the gentleman, advancing as he spoke, set polished riding boot on the lower stair, — a sleek though resolute foot this — whereat Bob made as if to oppose his further progress but, meeting these keen eyes, thought better of it and led the way up forthwith, and halting at last, rapped on and opened a dingy, time-scarred door.

"Your honour," said he, "gen'leman to see ye!"

But even as he spoke, a masterful hand set him aside and the gentleman in question stood upon the threshold. Now the room was well-lighted and thus Bob was enabled to see this gentleman's face very distinctly, beholding which, he started, pursed his lips as if about to whistle but, instead of so doing, turned suddenly and sped away down the stair and for once, it was to be noted, his heavy boots clattered not at all. Reaching a certain dark archway he paused there and whistled softly; and lo! presently in that place of gloom were dim forms, sinister shapes that moved on feet of velvet and spake him in sibilant whispers, that shrank to stealthy, crouching shadows, blotches in the gloom very still, very silent, patiently expectant.

Mr. Willoughby-Gafton was drinking wine in company with the ferocious Colonel Santerre and the debonair Vicomte de Villebois, but beholding his visitor he rose and bowed.

"You desire to see me, sir?" he enquired in French. "I am Henry Willoughby-Gafton."

Sir Peter stepped into the room, closing the door behind him.

"Sir," said he, "my name is Vibart."

Mr. Gafton's eyes narrowed suddenly, his brows twitched, then he smiled and bowed more profoundly than before.

"I am honoured!" said he. "You are perhaps Sir Peter Vibart, related to young Richard, — yes?"

"His father, sir."

"Ah — permit me! Messieurs," said he, addressing his companions, "I am charmed to present Sir Peter Vibart, baronet, sire to Monsieur Richard Vibart whom you know."

Hereupon Vicomte and Colonel rose to bow very ceremoniously.

"And now, Sir Peter, will you be seated?"

"Thank you, sir, I prefer to stand."

"Then permit that I have the happiness to fill for you a glass of wine, Sir Peter. . . . Hola, my Robinet, a glass here! Sacred name, where is the animal? Ha — Robert!"

"Pray do not trouble," said Sir Peter. "And if these gentlemen will excuse me, I will speak in English."

"Oh, by all means, Sir Peter, at your pleasure!" Here Mr. Gafton and his two companions bowed again, all three.

"I am here, sir," said Sir Peter, returning their salutations a little stiffly, "to ask on what conditions you will forego your meeting with my son, — having regard to his impetuous youth?"

"Alas!" sighed Mr. Gafton, shaking his head affectedly, "under no conditions, I fear."

"Having regard to my son's extreme youth?" reiterated Sir Peter.

"My dear sir, it is quite impossible, — the affair is all arranged — "

"That is why I am here."

"How extraordinary!" murmured Mr. Gafton. "And, permit me to say, how very irregular!"

"Sir, my son was just nineteen years old last month!"

"And a remarkably fine fellow for his age, Sir Peter."

"And, seeing he is indeed so very young, I come on his behalf to proffer such reparation as I may."

"Pray, sir, what do you mean by 'reparation'?"

"That is for you to define, sir."

"But, my dear Sir Peter, at your son's age I had 'been out' twice, I assure you."

"Possibly, sir. But then Richard is — my son!"

"Oh, perfectly!" nodded Mr. Gafton. "Yet your son was old enough to . . . strike me! And, sir, no one may so affront me with impunity."

"Not even a boy?"

"No one alive, Sir Peter, — no, not even — your son! Two days hence I must shoot him — oh, without fail, regrettable, but — my so outraged honour demands it."

"That," said Sir Peter, his lip curling, "that will be quite impossible."

"Sir, you amaze me! Why 'impossible', pray?"

"Because I shall not permit him to meet you."

"Death of my life!" exclaimed Mr. Gafton, and turning to his friends, he imparted to them this astonishing fact in rapid French.

"Ten thousand thunders!" quoth the Colonel, with restrained ferocity.

"Oh, but it is incredible!" cried the Vicomte. "No man of honour dare refuse a challenge. Ohé, the so grave English gentleman makes you the joke, Henri, and I see it, and I laugh, —" and the Vicomte laughed forthwith very youthfully while Sir Peter surveyed them all three with an austere curiosity.

Mr. Gafton emptied his glass thirstily and refilled it slowly.

"You think our gentleman is joking, Victor," said he, "but no, I assure you he is merely English and therefore of an arrogance." Here he emptied his glass again and turned smiling to his silent visitor. "Sir Peter," he laughed, "let us suppose the impossible, let us imagine that I forget this outrageous affront and forego calling your so cherished offspring to account, — how then?"

"You will have his parents' deep gratitude, sir."

"But the gratitude of parents does not interest me in the very least, Sir Peter."

"Then anything else, in reason!"

"Unfortunately, my dear Sir Peter, I was never reasonable."

"Mr. Gafton, you being a duellist so expert and infallible, might reasonably forego the shooting of an inexperienced boy, since none would question your motive."

"Perfectly!" murmured Mr. Gafton. "And yet, having regard to that blow . . . alas, sir, I fear the shooting must be . . . ! And yet again . . . perhaps . . . I might be dissuaded, or shall we say — persuaded to . . . spare your idolized son."

"Pray be more explicit, sir."

"Well — there is his . . . mother."

"Sir?"

"She might succeed where you fail."

"Indeed, Mr. Gafton?"

"A mother's eloquence, my dear Sir Peter! Indeed, I almost think I might be persuaded if she came pleading his cause . . . yes, she might perhaps win me to . . . reconsider the matter — "

"Lady Vibart is in England, sir."

"Well, she might be here in time, Sir Peter, — yes, I would even defer the encounter to suit her convenience."

Sir Peter's right hand clenched, a white yet very solid-looking fist, but his look and tone were serenely impassive as ever when he answered:

"Sir, such consideration for her touches me very sensibly!"

Mr. Gafton brimmed his glass, viewing the wine with eyes strangely bright and avid, also his cheeks showed unwontedly flushed and a faint tremor seemed to pass over him; then he smiled and bowed.

"Consideration?" he repeated. "Ah, but certainly — are we not all slaves to Beauty? And beauty such as hers might win a man to — anything! . . . And Charmian, Lady Vibart, as a supliant would be quite irresistible to any man, more especially to me who — "

Sir Peter leapt with straight-driving fist and, reeling from the blow, Mr. Gafton went down heavily; then Sir Peter's whip was flailing him — while the Vicomte watched with youthful glee and rubbed small hands, albeit furtively . . . until the Colonel, spluttering oaths, interposed.

Sir Peter, a little surprised at his own vehemence, tossed aside the whip, picked up his fallen hat, and reordered his attire with as much dignity as possible.

"Mr. Willoughby-Gafton," said he, having thus recovered his breath, "I venture to think this may suffice; if not, pray take notice this flogging shall be repeated as often and as publicly as possible."

Mr. Gafton arose and, somehow, contrived to do it with dignity and grace.

"Sir, you . . . win your point!" said he, between bloody lips. "Instead of callow son I will shoot devoted sire."

"Precisely!" said Sir Peter, smoothing the ruffled nap of his hat. "Now, at once, if you will — here, across the table or — "

"No!" answered Mr. Gafton, refilling the glasses with steady hand. "You shall wait my time, sir — you shall wait and — think! For at my time and convenience I shall most certainly shoot you dead."

Sir Peter bowed and went from the room and down the stair, a little grim and extremely dignified. Reaching the courtyard, he paused to glance up at the stars, viewing their palpitant glory with an odd sense of comradeship and well-being, then, a leisured, stately figure, he stepped into the sudden darkness of that gloomy archway . . . was seized by many griping hands, was pinioned, stifled, trussed into a helpless bundle and borne ingloriously away.

CHAPTER XII

CHARMIAN tossed aside the intricate needle-work she had been so vainly endeavouring to concentrate upon and staring into the fire that smouldered in the chimney, shuddered violently; for the air of this lofty *appartement,* high above the bustling street, seemed chill; moreover she was shaken, heart and soul, mind and body, by an ever-growing anxiety; the hands of her travelling clock, on the table beside her, crept so slowly while her perfervid imagination conjured up such dread visions of what might be happening at this moment . . . must indeed happen to this man who was part of herself . . . her very life. And now, as she crouched thus, racked by a suspense almost beyond even her powers of endurance, she breathed his name as it had been a prayer:

"Peter! Oh, my dear! It is for our love's sake! And my love is all about you! And God

is in heaven! But oh, the agony of waiting!
. . . Dear God, make me strong . . . teach
me a way, — the way!"

Starting to her feet, she paced the wide
apartment, head bowed and tremulous hands
clasped before her, hands that twisted and
wrung each other while her quick brain
wrought and wrought so desperately, scheming
some method to avert and outwit Merciless
Vengeance; plotting some means of salvation
for these menfolk of hers . . . how to trick
them, check and turn them aside from that
male-made path leading to what was termed
the Field of Honour (this swamp of blood and
tears) which she knew in her heart would but
lead them to their certain destruction.

"To find a way! Some way! The way! But
— how?" How with her woman's wit and feminine guile to checkmate determined, egre-
gious Masculinity?

Coming to the heavily curtained window,
she leaned there to think, — and think, resting
troubled forehead against the pane; and from
this eminence her anxious eyes looked down
upon and far across this great city of Paris, its

myriad lights sending up a pale radiance to a sombre heaven.

"To find a way; Some way! Any way!"

All at once above the vague, unceasing murmur that was the voice of this teeming hive of humanity, clocks near and far boomed, tinkled and whispered the hour.

Ten o'clock! Another hour sped and no nearer a solution! . . . To pit herself and all her resources, all that she was — against . . . She caught her breath and turned suddenly as the door opened and Miss Janet entered — to be leapt at, clasped, shaken and questioned in as many moments:

"Janet, is it done? Is he safe away? Oh, is he safe and unharmed? Well . . . well, — oh, speak!"

"Ay!" quoth Miss Janet, laying aside her weighty reticule and loosing her bonnet strings.

"Tell me, Janet! Tell me all. You were there in time? You saw . . . heard . . . everything?"

"I did that!"

"Oh, for heaven's sake, then — tell me, do!"

"My dear, there's vera little to tell," answered Miss Janet, seating herself on an ottoman and drawing Charmian beside her. "Ye see, Mr. Meadows and his villains were by-ordinar' dexterous, ou ay! And black masks m' dear, every one, like sae many bogles! Your Peter comes striding across yon courtyard very stately and dignified, ay — stalks intae yon dark archway like the proodest laird o' creation and comes oot o' yon archway like a sack o' potatoes — "

"Oh, Janet . . . you mean — "

"Ay, a sack o' potatoes, or coals, — larger mebbe and juist as helpless. Aweel, they dump the puir man intae a waiting *fiacre* and awa' wi' him — "

"Did he . . . oh, did he struggle . . . very much?"

"My dearie, sic question is fair ridiklous; ye ken fine he did — and himsel' Peter Vibart! Ay, frae the despret soonds I heard, I jalouse he strugglet!"

"Did he groan, Janet, as if — they'd hurt him? Did he cry out, did — "

"Na, na, — and himsel' always sae dignified!

Forbye he had sma' chance for it, ye see — his heid was in a bag — "

"A bag! Oh! But they didn't dare hurt him! Oh, Janet, he wasn't harmed . . . you are sure?"

"I'll no juist swear tae this, but — "

"Janet, if they've harmed him . . . one hair of his dear head — "

"No, no, my dear, Peter is none the worse — except in his dignity, of course! But . . . oh, Charmian, such wild, wild business! My dear, however could you — "

"Because it was one way, Janet, — the only way I could think of to save him from his own rash spirit and this . . . oh, this hateful Gentlemanly Code, — this vile, ridiculous business of — Honour! Death, death or dishonour that has ended and wasted so many splendid lives and broken so many hearts!"

"Ay!" nodded Miss Janet. "However, you've made your Peter safe — for the time being."

"Yes, thank God! But now . . . as regards Henry Gafton . . . the wicked, remorseless cause of it all. I must scheme out . . . some . . . other way, Janet! But the dear Lord help us . . . how? What? And the hours fleeting by so quickly, so — ah, there he is, I think!" said she, starting up as came a soft rapping at the door.

"He? Who?" cried Miss Janet, rising also. "Here . . . at this hour? Not — "

"Yes, the man Meadows, I think, for his . . . blood money. Open and let us see, my dear."

Striding to the door forthwith, Miss Janet flung it wide, discovering the squat, powerful form of Mr. Robert Meadows in person who, having bobbed his head at them, closed the door with that deft and neat precision that characterized him, and now, obedient to my lady's gesture, advanced into the room, thus showing a visage somewhat marred as by recent combat.

"Well, Mr. Meadows?"

"As any trivet, ma'm, except for this here ogle or, as you might say, peeper, m' lady."

"If you mean your eye," said Charmian, looking at the member in question with an almost prideful possessiveness, "I can see it quite plainly; it looks very swollen and inflamed. Did he . . . the gentleman — "

"He did, ma'am! He sartainly, sure-ly did! A flush left, m' lady — "

"Does it pain you?"

"Well, nothing to mention, ma'm. Ye see, I was in the P.R. once and very much fancied. But you was right, lady; he knows a bit, your gentleman, — floored me once, ah, and Pierre ditter."

"Yes, he is very strong, Mr. Meadows, but . . . you didn't . . . hurt him? You are sure he took no harm — "

"Bible oath, lady! We 'andles him like he had been glass, or very near."

"And you conveyed him to the lodging I showed you? You left him quite comfortable, with everything he can possibly need?"

"As any dook, emperor, markis, or grandee, lady! Two sarvants to wait on him, 'and and foot, — and, ah, lady — Françoise to cook for him, Françoise, ma'm, as is the primest chef — "

"Well, won't you sit down, Mr. Meadows?"

"Thankee, ma'm, but — "

"Oh, I have the money for you. See, it is all here!" And from a dainty handbag on the table

before her Charmian now drew notes and gold
— so much that Bob Meadows caught his
breath and blinked.

"Now won't you please sit down?" she repeated gently. "I won't keep you very long.
You see, I wish to explain certain matters to
you."

"Ma'm," he answered rather gruffly, "there
aren't no needs for no explanations nohow."

"I said I — wished to," said my lady gently
though firmly. Bob glanced about him rather
uneasily, — at curtained doorways and shady
corners, at Miss Janet sitting very grimly upright, at the lovely speaker and, murmuring
hoarsely, took the chair she indicated.

"Mr. Meadows," said she, leaning towards
him very graciously, "I am sure you will understand my great anxiety for the gentleman
you have just been abducting for me when I
tell you that he is my — very dear husband — "

"Eh, ma'm — " Bob Meadows half rose in
his astonishment, sank down again, shook his
head and ejaculated in feeble tones, "Blow
me!"

"And I chose you for this . . . oh, this — "

"Job o' work, lady?"

"Yes. I chose you, Mr. Meadows, because I knew you were such a very gentle, good man — "

"Eh — me, ma'm? Good? Gent — what . . . me?"

"Of course!" she answered, smiling at him very kindly. "Any man who could love a little child as devotedly as you love your little Nanette must be gentle and good. And this is why I am going to ask you to help me again."

"What . . . again, lady? Not another — "

"No, no. This is a matter quite different. Listen and you shall understand. I have come to France . . . to save two lives much dearer to me than my own . . ." Here, briefly though eloquently, Charmian explained the situation, while Bob Meadows, his shrewd eyes on her beautiful and animated face, listened speechlessly.

"Now, Mr. Meadows, my son Richard tells me that your master, Mr. Willoughby-Gafton, is the most dangerous man and deadly duellist in Paris."

"Yes, ma'm!" nodded Bob. "My Governor's sure death wits pistol or *epée,* no-torious, lady! Ah, and nobody to ekal him nohow — except, well, mebbe one other."

"Who? Pray, who is he?"

"Monsieur Victor, ma'm, the Vicomte de Villebois, lady; some think he's more deadly, but . . . I dunno."

"And . . . are they good friends, Monsieur le Vicomte and Mr. Gafton?"

"Ma'm, they takes precious good care to be — leastways the Vicomte does, but my Governor's the reckless, don't-care sort, fight him or any man any time or anywhere — just reckless, lady, and allus was."

"Well, I wish to meet this gentleman, this Monsieur Victor."

"What . . . the Vicomte?" exclaimed Bob, viewing the vivid beauty of her now with something very like horrified dismay. "Him, ma'm — you? No, no, he aren't fit to come a-nigh you."

"Now thank you," she murmured, her lovely eyes kinder than ever. "I am grateful to you for such thought! But I must meet him, none the less. You must contrive that I make his acquaintance to-morrow."

"No, madam — not me!" quoth Bob, rising.

"Wait!" said she, gesturing to the money on the table between them. "All this is yours according to our agreement. Well now, contrive me a meeting with Vicomte Victor and this two thousand louis d'or shall be three — "

"Three thousand!" Bob Meadows dropped his hat. "Three?" he gasped. "Lord! I'd do a'most anything for so much. . . . And yet — him and you! . . . If anything happened and through me . . . my little Nan might be blasted too . . . now or somewhen! No, ma'm — no! I can't! You dunno what you're asking! You dunno — his sort!"

"I think I do!"

"But no, Madame, no!" cried Bob, speaking now in rapid French, as if unable to find words for it in English. "I know this man, this Vicomte, his so vile, so great beastliness! He is to the Sex an animal — of an avidity, but yes! Of an uncleanness the most absolute!"

"And you, *mon ami*," she answered, rising impulsively and speaking in the same tongue, "show yourself a man so honourable that any woman helpless and distressed might trust. And Monsieur Bob, I am a woman and very, very distressed; help me, oh, my friend, help me in this!"

Here, smiling very wistfully, she reached him her hand. So Bob took this hand, holding it gently like the precious, lovely thing it was and answered in his most English manner:

"Lady," quoth he, squaring his mighty, prize-fighter's shoulders, "arter this 'ere there aren't nothing nor nobody in Paris shall do ee hurt or wrong while Bob Medders is a breathing soul! And what be more, there aren't nothing and nobody as I won't do for ee. As for money, ma'am, I'll take what's doo for sarvice rendered but for sarvice to be — not a sou!"

"Dear Bob Meadows!" she murmured. "As to more money, well — there is a cottage I know of in Sussex, and as for service to be it is this: I have written to Mr. Gafton, bidding him come at four o'clock to-morrow to a little house I have — here is the address on this paper; pray keep it — but instead of his visiting me, I shall call on him at half-past three and you must contrive that the Vicomte shall visit him also, say at a quarter to four or thereabouts. You will manage this for me, my friend?"

"Ay, I will, my lady, I will, and keep my eyes open too."

"Why, then, until to-morrow, good-bye!" said she, gathering up the notes of gold, "and with this money please accept the very deep and grateful thanks of a distressed woman."

Bob thrust the money into the breast of his much-darned, shabby genteel service coat, made to go and paused.

"My lady," said he, turning his hat round and round and staring into it very hard, "you have . . . honoured me . . . more than you know and . . . a sight more than I can ever tell ee. But actions speaks louder than words and so . . . p'raps some day . . . oh, well . . . *Bonne nuit, Mesdames!*" And bowing with all a Frenchman's grace but all his own sincere humility, he hurried away.

"Charmian," said Miss Janet, so soon as they were alone, "I do believe you could gentle roaring lions and tame bloodthirsty tigers!"

"Anything but snakes and reptiles, Janet."

"Snakes? Ah, — the Vicomte."

"Ah, don't mention him, my dear; sufficient unto the day! Come, let's go to bed."

"Yon Meadows man," said Miss Janet, as they disrobed before the fire, "yon ferocious creature that is a cross betwixt an Indian Thug, an English bulldog and a French bloody-minded Apache, had tears in his eyes and bowed to hide 'em — ay, he was greeting."

"Because yon Meadows man is a real man, Janet dear."

"And ready tae shed his blood for ye, Charmian."

"Which is a very comforting thought, my dear."

"Ay, but 'tis no this makes your een sae bright . . . like stars, my dear, and your cheeks a' flushed — why, Charmian, why?"

"Because," answered Charmian, staring down into the fire, her wide eyes bright with a fearful triumph, "I think . . . I have found . . . the Other Way!"

CHAPTER XIII

My Lady Charmian, her Method Feminine

MR. WILLOUGHBY-GAFTON, more resplendent than ever, having called down the usual bitter curses on his all too inadequate looking-glass, smiled complacently at his reflection, took up the dainty *billet doux* that stood propped against his sadly depleted pomatum pot and conned over the written message as he had done at intervals since it had reached him; and the words these:

"Lady Vibart presents her compliments to Willoughby-Gafton Esqr. and begs the favour of his attendance this afternoon at three o'clock on a matter very near her heart."

And below this, scribbled in the lower, left-hand corner:

"Do not fail me, Henry."

And in the lower right-hand corner:

"For the sake of other days."

And Mr. Gafton smiled, his handsome teeth looking very white and exceeding sharp.

"A damned alluring witch always!" he murmured and laughed gently. "Ah, well, since she stoops to the lure as expected, let us see — ! Robin," he called gaily, "Robinet, my faithful cabbage, behold five francs for thee! Nay, gape not, my fish, but bring me instantly my hat and the clouded amber cane. For to-day, my Rob, I go to bask in the smiles of beauty! To-day I — ha, malediction! I'll see nobody! Say I'm out!" he exclaimed pettishly, for now was a knocking at the outer door: crossing thereto, Bob swung it wide and with rustle of silk and whispering stir of petticoats, Charmian entered.

And surely never did blue poplin shadow forth such alluring beauties as this same gown that clasped her shapeliness in such caressing folds; never did coquettish bonnet frame more lovely face, as she stood, a little flushed and something breathless, all vivid and aglow with quick-breathing life.

Mr. Gafton actually forgot to bow, and was silent so long that she questioned him at last:

"You can guess why I am here?"

"Charmian . . ." he breathed.

"At least ask me to sit down, Henry."

He placed a chair for her with hands not quite steady and stood looking down on her with the same rapt expression.

"I saw you a year ago in London from a distance," said he, in tone that matched his look. "I thought you beautiful then . . . to-day you are divine! The years do but glorify you, Charmian."

"Nay, this is fulsome!" said she, opening her fan, "and the day so hot and trying!"

"Shall I open another window?"

"No, pray be seated and let us talk." Mutely he obeyed and sat viewing her speechlessly.

"Well," she demanded at last, meeting his look with her calm, level gaze, "Well, Henry, when do you propose to kill my husband?"

Mr. Gafton's eyes wavered, grew hard and bright and he laughed softly.

"All in good time!" he murmured. "It is a prospect I dwell upon. After all, life has its little compensations."

"Compensations?" she repeated, in voice

softly modulated as his own. "You were always vindictive, Henry, even as a boy, and Sir Peter struck you, I believe?"

"He was so ill-advised! A rash being who seems positively eager to destroy himself, for, alas, I have no recourse but to — shoot him! Therefore, my dear soul, if you come to plead for him pray do not, and thus spare me the pain of refusal."

"Henry, I am told that you shoot very well."

"Tolerably, I believe."

"Almost as well as your notorious friend, the Vicomte de Villebois."

"Quite as well, I venture to think."

"And you have killed men in duels?"

"Occasionally, alas!"

"Though not so many as your friend the Vicomte, perhaps."

"I believe the dear Victor has been more unfortunate than myself upon two occasions, but I may have the unhappiness to equal him ere long — who knows?"

"Yes, Henry, — having threatened my dear son's life, you would kill my husband. Am I right in assuming that you are striking at me through those that I love? Though, indeed, I know it!" said she, watching him above her gently swaying fan, — his glittering, half-closed eyes, his sharp-toothed smile.

"But, now really, Charmian, can you possibly love that dignified austerity that calls itself Sir Peter Vibart — you? By Heaven, I refuse to credit such ridiculous impossibility. You so passionately alive — and he — ? Indeed, I have thought the worthy gentleman would look his best in marble — on a tomb, say."

"And your age, Henry, is forty-five!"

"Forty-four, Charmian."

"Forty-five!" she repeated. "I wonder you have survived so long."

"Indeed?"

"Yes. It surprises me that no one has killed you long ago." Mr. Gafton laughed gaily and leaned back in posture of indolent grace.

"Does the wish father the thought, I wonder?" he sighed. "Ah, well, several misguided unfortunates have attempted my — translation hence, yet I have been preserved for this happy hour, Charmian, this very charming occasion."

"How right was my childish detestation of you, Henry! And I never feared you; I never shall."

"For this, at least, I am grateful."

"To-day I pity you for what you are and — what you might have been. I mean the waste of faculties that should have made you a — less ignoble creature."

Once again his bold eyes wavered, his pale cheek flushed painfully and his soft laughter rang a little false.

"And you, my Lady Charmian, upon my soul, you are scarcely so humble, so tremulously diffident as a suppliant is generally supposed."

"I do not come to supplicate, Henry."

"No?" he enquired, masking his surprise.

"Indeed no!"

"Then pray, what was the meaning of your — engagingly intimate note? Why are you here — alone with me, Charmian?"

"To bargain," answered my lady.

Mr. Gafton sat up with a jerk, then, very slowly, leaned towards her to stare . . . and stare in dumb yet avid question; but reading her answer in the eyes that met his with such serene and utterly passionless gaze, his eager fingers, that had crept so near her own, clenched suddenly to quivering fist.

"Did the worthy Sir Peter send you to me, Madame?" he demanded hoarsely. My lady merely curled disdainful lip, then she smiled faintly and shook her head in tolerant reproof:

"How clumsy, Henry! But then, you are angry."

Mr. Gafton frowned blackly, laughed stridently and bowed.

"*Touché!*" he nodded. "A palpable hit! Egad, Sir Peter is no complaisant spouse; I ask his dignified pardon. You are here, of course, without his knowledge — delightful fact!"

"Of course, Henry."

"And such sweet stealth, Charmian! So deliciously secretive! Yes, despite your arrogant pride and wifehood, you have crept to me at last — because I willed it so, have fled across sea and land — to my delight."

"Are you making love to me, Henry?"

"Is there any need, Charmian? In your letter here," and he tapped the breast of his coat, "you write: 'for the sake of other days.' Well, let us recall those days. Lay by your dignity, forget your pride, — blush, sigh, tremble, — look at me again with the shy-bold eyes of questioning sixteen, for one little hour be as you were that day you kissed me, twenty-odd years ago — God knows it was all innocent enough!"

"Yes, — it was — twenty-odd years ago!" she answered. "You were my boyish lover. . . . But you went away to the university and came back — a man, and hatefully changed —"

"No, an adoring boy still!"

"A hateful boy that I detested. . . . And then, you forged your uncle's name —"

"Admitted!" smiled Mr. Gafton.

"You attempted his life —"

"No, — that is false! That I utterly deny!"

"You suggested as much in the letter you wrote me before you fled."

"It is quite possible," he nodded, "yes, it is even probable, for I would have damned myself with all the cardinal sins to show the deeps I'd sound, the lengths I'd go, the heights I'd

climb to win you — in those days, Charmian.
I was a wild, reckless boy and you — ah, you
were my immaculate siren, wooing me to ruin
and despair, my ever-chaste and beautiful de-
stroyer, my always-virtuous lure to evil,
my — "

"Stop, stop!" she cried. "For shame! Your
ruin was your own wild and wicked nature.
To blame others is the act of a weak craven!
However, that most compromising letter was
not destroyed — "

"Aha, sweet Venus bless thee! Can it be that
it was cherished for sake of the once-loved,
cruelly jilted, miserable writer? What — no?
I thought not!"

"No, Henry. I would have destroyed it but
— it was snatched from the fire and preserved
all these years without my knowledge until re-
cently."

"Well, Charmian, and what then?"

"My husband's life for this letter."

Mr. Gafton's face darkened; then he smiled,
leaned back in his chair and laughed, while my
lady, fanning herself gently, watched him with
curious eyes.

"Do you find it so amusing?" she enquired at last.

"Oh, beyond expression!" he answered, laughing still. "Oh, my bewitching black-mailer! Most virtuous stately dame, is this your sorry bargain?"

"Why, what — what do you mean?" said she, a little breathlessly.

"I mean, my haughty lady, that the inept sinning of the foolish boy touches the man no whit. Publish the miserable letter by all means, print it in the journals, paste it on the walls, score it upon the sky, for all I care. . . . No, my Lady Charmian, disdainful, heartless witch, — as I once pleaded, wept, grovelled in my abasement, so must you supplicate, if you will, upon your proud knees, Madame, beseeching me with sobs and tears and every line of that beautiful body, and then . . . well, perhaps I may be moved to consider the possibility of handing your stately spouse back to your arms — merely blooded, — winged but — alive."

Charmian closed her fan and sat, with head adroop, staring blankly down at it; mute she remained thus and so very still that Mr. Gafton began to fidget and rising suddenly, crossed to the open window and leaned there a while.

"Well," he demanded at last, "what now?"

"I am praying, Henry."

"Death of my life!" he muttered.

"You believed in prayer — once, Henry. I do still. . . . I am praying to find — another way."

Then he was before her, shaken from his cynical calm at last, his eyes bright with fierce anger, his mouth bitterly scornful as he frowned down into her paling face.

"Ah, Charmian," said he between shut teeth, "oh, Immaculate Chastity that would dare ask all and give nothing, — Impeccable Virtue that, still immaculate, would triumph by a trick — yourself as immune as ever, Madame, — well now, save your darling by your holy prayers — if you can! For by God, Madame, any gentleness I may have cherished for you even yet, any mercy I might have shown for the sake of those other days, I cast from me — there, they are dead and done with . . . the life that hangs upon my trigger-finger shall be snuffed out — pray how you will!"

"I am . . . praying now . . . Henry!" she whispered brokenly, clasping her hands like one in agony.

. . . And then the door swung open and Vicomte Victor entered with youthful exuberance but, espying Charmian, halted suddenly, opened his so innocent eyes very wide, bowed profoundly and stood viewing her vivid loveliness, his youthful air strangely at odds with his eyes — eyes of a gloating satyr in the face of a plump, rosy cherub.

"Ah," he murmured, "a thousand pardons! Is it that I intrude — yes, no?"

"In effect, my dear Victor, you do!" answered Mr. Gafton a little stiffly.

"Alas!" sighed the Vicomte, his burning gaze still fixed. "My Henri, I am desolated, but the . . . the affair is of moment and — "

"Then pray keep it for — some other moment, Victor."

Here, slowly and unwillingly, the Vicomte turned to glance at the speaker.

"But, Monsieur Henri, I am then *de trop?*"

he murmured, his slim, delicate brows slightly lifted.

"Perfectly, Monsieur the Vicomte!" answered Mr. Gafton, his thick brows close-knit. And then my lady, quick to heed and take advantage of this flash of sudden antagonism, spoke in her most dulcet tones:

"Pray Henry, present your friend."

Ungraciously and almost awkwardly Mr. Gafton complied, whereupon the Vicomte tripped forward and lifting her hand to his eager lips, kissed it with a lingering rapture while she saluted him with a curtsey particularly gracious. And then once again the door swung wide and young Richard stood upon the threshold, flushed, breathless and a little wild.

"Mother," he cried in petulant anxiety, "Madame, I . . . I could wait no longer! Let me take you away —"

"Ah!" said Mr. Gafton, quite unheeding the distraught youth, "So, Charmian, even your visit was not so sweetly furtive as you gave me to suppose!"

"Mother," cried Richard, striding into the

room, "let me escort you from here . . . and if this . . . this fellow has dared affront you—"

"Hush, Richard! You should know I do not suffer myself to be affronted. Pray leave me, go back and wait me at the hotel."

"But, Mother—"

"Go, Richard! Monsieur le Vicomte shall escort me to the carriage."

"Ah, Madame," cried the Vicomte, bowing in a very transport, "but with a joy the most intense!"

Hereupon, meeting his mother's compelling gaze, Richard turned and still flushed and a little wilder than ever, strode out and away.

Then my lady arose and giving her hand to the Vicomte's fervid clasp, went forth upon his arm, leaving Mr. Gafton to gnaw at scarlet nether lip and scowl darkly at the worn and dingy carpet.

From these bitter reflections he was roused at last by the hoarse voice of Bob Meadows:

"By your leave sir, I'd like to-night off."

Sinking into worn armchair, master surveyed man with languid yet grave curiosity:

"What — again, my Lothario?" he murmured. "Alas, you too! Beware of the women, my faithful cabbage, — tigers and cats, death and damnation! Is it understood?"

"Ar! They don't mean nothing to me, sir."

"Why then, you may bring me the cognac." Bob obeyed with that speed and precision of movement so very evident at times. "And now," said Mr. Gafton, pouring the brandy, "suppose you confess what takes you abroad so often of late."

But while Bob was meditating suitable answer and before his master could raise glass to lip, the door burst violently open and young Richard was back again, still breathless but looking wilder than ever. With a certain youthful exaggeration of gesture he closed the door, locked it and faced Mr. Gafton, pale, trembling and desperately grim:

"Sir," said he, steadying his voice with an effort, "I come to demand instant and final settlement of . . . of our difference . . . at once . . . this moment!" And from the folded cloak upon his arm he produced two pistols, one of which he laid upon the table and, with the other gripped in tense fingers, stepped back, facing Mr. Gafton across the wide hearth.

And now ensued a pause, wherein Richard fidgeted nervously while Mr. Gafton, lolling at ease, sipped his brandy and surveyed the set young face opposite with lazy interest.

"Robinet, my old one," he murmured at last, "our young gentleman is not drunk, surely? Let us hope not for his handsome mother's sake — "

"Mr. Gafton," cried Richard, between trembling lips, "I forbid you to mention her . . . my mother! Get up, sir — take that pistol, or this — make your choice and let us be done! Your man there shall give the count. Stand up, I say!"

"Robin, my small cabbage," sighed Mr. Gafton wearily, "desire the so agitated young gentleman to depart at once and vapour elsewhere."

"Silence, sir!" cried Richard. "I am beyond your sneers. Pick up that pistol . . . I . . . I am ready to answer for the blow I struck you — no one else shall, I swear. So arm yourself . . . stand up, I say, or by God I'll shoot you as you sit — take up that pistol! Don't . . . don't drive me too far, Gafton," he panted. "Oh, you fool, don't you see, can't you understand? I'll kill you or be killed — gladly . . . I'd murder you to save my father!" And stepping forward, he levelled weapon at his tormentor's mocking face. . . . Mr. Gafton sipped his brandy.

The pistol wavered in Richard's grasp, he drew a sobbing breath and wiped sweat from his pallid face.

"Sir," said he in strange, hushed voice, "I'll count five and fire. One! . . . Two! . . . Three — "

With that self-same speed and precision of motion Bob Meadows leapt and struck with expert fist and so accurately that Richard went down headlong and lay inert. Indeed he lay so very still that Mr. Gafton troubled himself to lean forward and peer down into that pale, young face.

"Egad, Bob," he exclaimed in English, his languor quite forgotten, "you never struck sweeter blow even in the prize ring!"

"Ar!" nodded Bob, glancing down at his

handiwork with appraising eye. "He won't trouble nobody for a bit, your honour — "

"Excellent, my faithful one! Accept my thanks and these base ten francs, also thy leave of absence is granted, — begone, Robinet, and take our slumberous young gentleman with thee."

"Ay, but wheer, sir?"

"Anywhere for me, Robin, but for him I suggest his lady mother. . . . A lad of a recklessness this, Robinet, a youth of a determination extreme, for — death of my life, I believe he would have shot me indeed."

"I'm pretty surely sartin of it, your honour."

"Then why prevent him, my small, old one?"

"Why, sir," answered Bob, giving his moustache a sudden tug, "since you asks me, I dunno."

"And damme, Bob," said Mr. Gafton, reverting to English, "everything considered — neither do I."

CHAPTER XIV

Has the Merit of Being Short

THUS, to an aristocratic little house situated in an highly aristocratic (though discreetly retired) little thoroughfare, a speeding hackney coach bore young Richard still sublimely unconscious, and beside him the grim cause thereof, namely and to wit, Mr. Robert Meadows who, knowing exactly how and where his unerring, powerful and much-experienced fist had struck, evinced neither surprise nor disquiet at his victim's protracted unconsciousness.

The hackney coach or *fiacre* now turning aside into the high-bred quietude of a small though dignified forecourt, pulled up; whereupon Mr. Meadows, descending, pulled a bell which summons was duly answered by a grave-faced person in rich yet sober livery, to whom Bob forthwith addressed himself, in French so forcible and with gestures so eloquent and altogether compelling that he was promptly ushered into the presence of my lady and Miss Janet.

"Mesdames!" said he, saluting them; and then "My lady," quoth he, fumbling with his hat but meeting her questioning look with gaze unflninching, "I've got your young gentleman son outside in a *fiacre*."

"But why here, Mr. Bob? Why not the Soleil d'Or?"

"Why, you see, my lady, I — well, I thought it best under the circumstances, ma'm, 'considering.'"

"Considering what, pray?"

"That he aren't able to walk-like, him not being exackly for the moment what you might call 'all there' nor yet *compus mentus,* ma'm."

"Not — oh, Bob Meadows, what has happened now — ?"

"Only a blow, my lady, or as you might say a 'bender' or 'wallop', ma'm. You see your young gentleman son aforesaid, my lady, was a'going to shoot my Governor, so I were compelled to let him have it, ma'm, — jest once, my lady, but in the proper place, which put him to sleep sweet and innocent as any smiling babe, ma'm."

"Hoot-toot, man!" exclaimed Miss Janet severely. "D' ye tell us the puir wean's no' conscious?"

"Ar, ma'm. Shall I bring him in?"

"First . . . oh, quickly tell all that happened — quickly!" cried my lady.

"Well, Mesdames, your Mr. Richard comes in to my Governor like a wild man. . . . Pistols! Two on 'em! Tries to force my Governor to fight him there and then — across the hearth, ladies — on account of his father —"

"Oh, the dear, mad boy!"

"But my Governor only laughs. Then Mr. Richard says as how to save his father he'll murder my Governor, levels a pistol, threatens to fire and, well — I drops him, my lady, as aforesaid, ma'm. Shall I bring him in here?"

"No, carry him upstairs; he shall go to bed —"

"Bed, my lady? No, no, there aren't no call for no bed. Lord bless ee, a douche o' cold water and he'll be right and bright as a —"

"However, friend Bob, you will please carry him up to bed, you and one of the footmen — "

"Nay, I'll manage him, easy, ma'm, easy!" quoth Bob and sped away incontinent.

"Now blessings on my Bob Meadows!" cried Charmian. "Richard shall instantly to bed — and stay there out of harm's way! Richard shall be sick, my dear, an invalid with a doctor in attendance — old Doctor Dupin, you remember him, Janet? Go, go and bring him here at once, if possible. I shall confide in him and Richard shall be our dear invalid; yes — he shall be dosed if need be! So bring me Doctor Dupin, there is a *fiacre* at the door, I think; now go, Janet — go!"

Miss Janet frowned, sighed, shook her head but — departed.

Thus it was that, after some while, Richard opened his eyes to a sponge, very large and moist, wielded by my lady's capable hand; also he was amazed and mortified to find himself in bed.

"Good heavens," he began indignantly, "why am I — "

Here the sponge silenced him what time my

lady, sighful though stern, lashed him with reproaches:

"Oh, disobedient, wicked boy! Oh, to have deceived me so hatefully, — stealing away so soon as my back was turned!"

"But, Mother — "

"Be silent, sir! Do not seek to justify yourself! Ah, surely no poor soul was ever so plagued by her wilful, headstrong men-folk! Heaven help me!"

"But dear Mother, I — "

"Richard — hush! I'll hear no excuses. I expressly forbade you even attempting to see Mr. Gafton — "

"Ah, then — you know — "

"Of course I do. I know that in your mad folly you actually . . . threatened murder and but for the man Meadows — oh, heaven only knows what fearful thing you might have done . . . rash, wretched boy!"

"Madam," retorted young Richard, eluding the sponge and speaking with as much dignity as possible, "do pray believe that I am not a boy. This quarrel with Mr. Gafton was mine and I am man enough to — "

"To break your mother's heart, ruin her life, blast her happiness, plunge her into untimely grave — hold your wicked head still — do!" Richard obeyed perforce and suffered her to sponge his swollen jaw, the large contusion and very small cut above his temple, to frown and sigh at him as she would.

But at last, blinking through water and despite dabbing sponge, he ventured to question her, though in all humility:

"Tell me . . . pray . . . what of . . . my father? Why did he go away . . . so suddenly and . . . where?"

"As I have told you before, Richard — hold still, sir! Your father went because—he was forced . . . compelled by . . . er . . . circumstances."

"But at such a time, Mother?"

"Exactly, Richard. Time was the important factor."

"But what business could — " The sponge stopped further utterance.

"Your father will return safe and well, bless him, so soon as he can. . . . And now the bandages for your poor head."

"Bandages?" cried Richard, recoiling. "But my dear mother — "

"And yet, no. I'll wait for the doctor — "

"Doctor? Heavens and earth, Mother I'm perfectly well. . . . I'm merely bumped. I've taken worse than this many a time . . . the cut is nothing — nothing indeed — "

"Calm yourself, Richard, or we shall have you in a fever — "

"But I don't need a doctor — "

Here Miss Janet opened the door to say the doctor had arrived at last.

"Thank Heaven!" quoth my lady fervently and, having posted Miss Janet beside the amazed, protesting Richard's bed, she went forth to interview the physician — a small, cheery gentleman he, who greeted her like the old friend he was and to whom my lady spoke in hushed yet eager accents and to such effect that the smiling and obliging gentleman having examined Richard very thoroughly, his bruises, his pulse, his tongue, became very grave, shook his head ominously and declared the invalid must remain in bed for three days at least.

Then, leaving Richard more amazed and indignant than ever, he hurried out and, alone with my lady, bowed and smiled to her grateful acknowledgments.

"So, dear Madame," he chuckled, "that should keep your so rash young gentleman quiet for a while, oh, beyond doubt."

"And you'll come again, dear Dr. Dupin, soon and often."

"But certainly, dear my lady. Monsieur Richard shall be your *malade imaginaire.*"

CHAPTER XV

TELLS HOW CHARMIAN PLAYED A PART

BENEATH a Louis Quinze ceiling whereon smiling Loves hurled roses at a plump and very naked Venus, sat my lady, glancing with a strange anxiety at the clock upon the heavily carven mantelpiece, a small clock balanced somewhat precariously on the opulent hip of a nude, gilded nymph, a clock with a soft, irregular tick that raced, now and then, like the beat of a frightened heart.

And my Lady Vibart's heart was like the clock, in that it also seemed to race and leap as she sat there so utterly still, listening — listening, her every sense on the alert, though to all outward seeming she was her most serene and gracious self.

Nevertheless so intent was she that when the door behind her opened suddenly, a door garnished by roguish cherubs, she started violently, though her eyes, wide with momentary apprehension, beheld no one more formidable than Miss Janet, bonnet on head and bulky reticule on arm, who halting suddenly, glared up and around at walls and ceiling of this small, luxurious boudoir; she eyed the roguish cherubs, scowled at Venus and snorted instant abhorrence:

"My certie!" she exclaimed. " 'Tis an awful room this! The mair I see it the waur it grows. Charmian, it's fair shamefu'! Heart alive, my dear, it's the house of a wanton!"

"Indeed, I believe it was once, Janet. This is why I've taken it, servants, carriages, horses — for a month. Though God forbid I should need it so long!"

"Ay! And who'll ye be expecting? Why must ye jump and look sae guilty?"

"Lord, Janet, don't be a fool!"

"It's no myself is the fool, I'm thinkin'. Tell me, what desperate, shameful risks are ye running—"

"No more than any other loving woman would take—"

"Ay! Then ye're expecting to meet—him again! And—here!"

"I expect Henry Gafton in about three quarters of an hour."

"No, not Henry Gafton; he's had enough, o' conscience, no, — I mean that little, evil, plump thing, that wee, foul creature calls itself Viscount Vileboy."

"And a most apt name for him, Janet dear," said my lady, with a rather wan smile. "I am expecting the little Vicomte in about ten minutes or so."

"But the man's a vile . . . beast! And the way he looks at you! Oh, Charmian!"

My lady glanced at the clock and shivered.

"Yes," she murmured, "yes . . . I know!"

"Then why permit his visits and — in such place? Why endure such — contamination?"

"No, Janet, only — disgust. And it is to a good purpose . . . this is The Way! The Other Way. The Apostle Paul says he fought with beasts at Ephesus, — well, I'm fighting with beasts here in Paris and in cause as righteous."

"But Charmian, my own dearie-heart, why? Why such vile way?"

"Because I see no other."

"Ah!" sighed Miss Janet. "Ah, but there is! Ay, there is so!" My lady glanced furtively at the reticule Miss Janet's powerful hands were fondling.

"How — how do you mean?" she questioned.

"No matter," answered Miss Janet, with a grim nod, "only I thank the guid Lord I'm here tae protect ye."

"Surely God can do that unaided, my dear."

"Mebbe! Ou, ay, I'll no deny His omnipotence, — forby it comforts me tae ken myself the instrument o' proveedence — if need be."

"Oh, Janet," sighed my lady wearily, "oh, my dear, you become almost as much a worry as my two headstrong, blundering men-folk."

"Ay, but Charmian, ye're so mysterious. What's to be the end? What are you scheming for — aiming at?"

Here, instead of answering, my lady glanced at the clock and shivered again, as with discreet knock on the door a very superior young footman appeared to enquire:

"Would Madame see a person one Robert Medo?"

"Mr. Meadows? Ah, but yes, immediately."

So in came Bob who, knuckling an eyebrow to the ladies, glanced at the splendour about him uneasily and catching sight of the Venus overhead, instantly abased his glance and fumbled with his hat.

"Well?" cried my lady, rising eagerly. "How is he to-day? How does he look? Does he eat well? Is he sleeping regularly? Is he quite, quite well? Speak, man, oh, friend Bob — speak!"

"Why, ma'm," answered Bob, somewhat bemused, "all as I can say to all that 'ere is — ar!"

"What, oh, what do you mean by 'ah'?"

"I means, lady, as he's right as a trivet, right as ninepence, couldn't be no better nohow — except his temper like."

"The dear soul! Is he angry?"

"Angry, ma'm? Lady, no gentleman couldn't never be, no, nor never was no angrier — "

"Yes, yes — of course! He would be — "

"Ma'm, — 'e is!"

"Otherwise he is quite well? Quite comfortable — and safe? You are sure?"

"And sartin, my lady! And how is t' other one, the young gen'leman, ma'm?"

"Very well, thanks to you, Mr. Meadows."

" 'Oping, ma'm, as you don't think as I walloped 'im too 'ard-like."

"No, oh, no!" answered my lady, between laugh and sob.

"Ye see, lady, me fists is a bit nobbly-like."

Came sudden rustle of silken draperies and, to Bob's speechless surprise, the fist in question was clasped and held between two slim, white hands.

"Yes," said Charmian, giving that same fist a tender little squeeze, "yes, it is very . . . nobbly-like, Mr. Meadows, and thank God for it! I'm grateful, — deeply, humbly grateful to it!" And she looked up from this powerful fist to the grim, fiercely moustachioed face through glittering tears. "For just because of this strong fist my dear son is alive and guiltless of bloodshed. . . . Ah, Janet, go back to him or we may have him flourishing more pistols, — go, my dear — " Even as she spoke the young footman reappeared to announce:

"Monsieur le Vicomte de Villebois!"

And, as Miss Janet vanished behind the cherub door, the Vicomte tripped gaily into the room, then halted to goggle at the imperturbable Bob beneath faintly wrinkling brows, a small, delicately perfumed creature, sleekly elegant and blooming with rosy youth.

"Alas, Madame, alas!" sighed he, "I speed myself hither on the wings of joy, hoping to find thee — all alone!" My lady smiled and dismissing Bob with a kindly nod, gave her hand to the Vicomte who, casting himself on his knees, covered it with ardent kisses, — he pressed it to his heart, he sighed, he languished until, the hand becoming somewhat restive, he rose and conducted her to a gilded ottoman and, there seated beside her, he sighed, ogled and languished more soulfully than ever.

"Ah, my goddess so adorable," he cried in piping, youthful accents, "I have existed but for this moment!"

"Really, Vicomte," she answered lightly, yet drooping her lashes to the persistent stare of his china-blue eyes, "you overwhelm me."

"Ah, Madame, I protest I think of you — oh, but constantly! Of thee I dream waking

and asleep, *oh, la, la!* But now — Henri Gafton his man, why do I find him here?"

"Henri Gafton is an old friend of mine."

"Ah, the so happy, so fortunate Henri! But
then, dear Madame, for myself I dream of a
happiness more great — a rapture — "

"Henri is also a friend of yours, Vicomte, is
it not so?"

"But yes," answered the Vicomte, shrugging
his narrow shoulders, "we agree, the good
Henri and I. We agree to — agree!"

"Yes, truly," murmured my lady, opening
and shutting her fan, "most people find it —
wisest to agree with Henri Gafton, I understand."

"Wisest, Madame, wisest? Sacred heaven —
why, pray?"

"He is a duellist so notorious . . . so
deadly!"

"But dear Madame, there are others, oh, my
faith yes, one or two — especially one! Certainly our Henri has a reputation, oh, beyond
a doubt, a fame second only to — "

"Ah, yes — yes!" cried my lady. "He is terrible, oh terrible! This is why I so fear him,

why I went to supplicate him on my son's behalf."

"Alas, your son!" cried the Vicomte, rolling his eyes in ecstatic commiseration. "The youth so gallant! Child heroic! So young, — *la, la!* For Henri is indeed of a ferocity, a dexterity infernal, a skill undeniable and second only to — one! One who is of a spirit so sublimely bold to forbid and defy even him . . . if — "

"One?" breathed my lady, viewing the little Vicomte, her lovely eyes wide in eager question.

"One, but certainly!" he answered, leaning nearer with smiling complacency. "One, my most beautiful, who lives but to serve and adore, who dreams ever of those so glorious eyes — myself!"

My lady sighed hopelessly and shook her bewitching head.

"Ah, yes," she murmured, "but Henri is so tall, so commanding, so hatefully assured, so determined, so strong and terrible . . . and you, Vicomte, you may be very brave and gallant . . . but . . ." here she turned away, sighing more hopelessly than ever.

"Oh — oh?" cried the Vicomte in shrill amazement. "But, Madame, — so? Well, pray what mean you by your 'but'?"

"Only that you are not commanding, or tall, or — "

The Vicomte leapt afoot, arms, legs, hands and eyes passionately protestant.

"Name of a name!" cried he, youthful figure very upright, slim brows close knit, eyes viciously bright, "how, Madame, how? Is it that you adore the great, gross animals then, — bulk, Madame, the cumbersome monsters, yes? But reflect, death of my soul, reflect! Our Napoleon was not the huge fellow, *sapristi* — no! Caesar was not the giant, and I, Madame, I am—Victor de Villebois!" And, smiting himself on small bosom, the Vicomte folded his arms with a magnificent gesture. My lady glanced at him, sighed, shook her head and — looked away again.

"Yes!" said she.

Now reading the cold disparagement in her look the Vicomte stood a moment speechless and utterly astounded; then, with hissing intake of breath, he moved very suddenly and she was struggling in his arms — arms that crushed with unexpected power while close and closer leered the eyes of a triumphant satyr.

"Fear me — yes!" he whispered. "Hate me — perhaps! But scorn me — no! I am — Victor!"

Desperately she held him off . . . until her strength began to fail . . . until the cherub door swung open and a large hand clutched him . . . spun him round and clapped a pistol to his breast.

"Doon wi' ye!" cried Miss Janet fiercely. "Doon on y'r wee hunkers and pray for the black and sinfu' soul o' ye!" The Vicomte blinked at the threatening weapon, gaped at the stern face behind it and recoiled as, closing her eyes, Miss Janet pulled the trigger.

But instead of expected deadly explosion came a faint click and opening her eyes Miss Janet stared at the useless pistol in speechless dismay . . . then, hand on bosom, the Vicomte bowed; and Charmian spoke:

"No, Janet, it won't go off because, you see, I had the charge drawn, a loaded pistol is so unsafe! . . . Go now, my dear, go back to our

Richard. I need no leaden bullets to protect me —"

Miss Janet let fall the pistol and covering her face, was shaken by a storm of violent sobs. . . . But Charmian's loving arms were about her and Charmian's gentle strength had brought her to the door, there to comfort and cherish, to kiss and whisper awhile; and so, without a word or backward glance, Miss Janet sped away. Then, closing the door, my lady turned.

"Monsieur the Vicomte," said she softly, "a small body may hold a great soul, but you, Monsieur, are so very pitifully small! Be good enough to leave me."

"My so beautiful one," he murmured, smiling and radiantly unabashed, "myself I am Victor and soon — ah, my faith, yes, this Victor shall teach thee how —" He checked and turned swiftly as the demure young footman presented himself once more and bowing spoke in tone discreetly modulated:

"Will Madame see Monsieur Henri Gafton?"

"No — yes, when I ring!" she answered

breathlessly; no sooner was the door shut than, her stately dignity seemingly forgotten, she became a shaken, timid, imploring creature.

"This terrible man!" she gasped. "So cold and merciless! Yet I . . . I must see him — " The Vicomte smiled and flourished.

"Courage, my most adorable, courage!" said he, posturing. "For behold I, Victor, am beside thee!"

"Ah, pray, Vicomte, do not let him find you here . . . wait — wait in this room, I beg — he shall not stay long. Wait — here!" And with agitated gesture she opened the little cherub door.

"My goddess," cried the Vicomte, soaring from passion of anger to ecstasy of triumph, "I comprehend — oh, perfectly! I am ravished — to the soul! I will wait, ah, yes, in a rapture transporting. See, I but kiss thy so lovely hand — now my hat, my cane — behold, I am gone, to return when you will!" And with a graceful pirouette he vanished behind the soft-closing cherub door.

Alone thus, my lady stood quick-breathing, hands clenched and eyes wide in terrified stare like one who stood upon the very brink of horror; suddenly she glanced up and around as though seeking some avenue of escape; then, crossing to the mantel, she rang the bell with fingers that twitched and quivered upon the silken cord.

And yet — when Mr. Gafton entered, he found her demurely busied with needle and tambour frame, seated upon an ottoman farthest removed from the cherub door. Laying by his hat he stood drawing off his gloves with quick, pettish motions, his thick brows knit darkly, while she, head bowed above her embroidery, watched him furtively ere she rose to greet him, placid and serene as usual.

"This is kind of you, Henry," said she.

"Indeed, I think it is," he retorted, and turned to view her with the same dark look; "yes, Charmian, all things considered, it is more than kind, for I come to advise you as a friend."

"Then," said she, taking up her embroidery again, "you may sit down, Henry." But instead of so doing, he paced restlessly to and fro while she stitched placidly with dexterous needle.

"First of all," said he, pausing suddenly, "you asked me here, I imagine, to apologise for your son's wild conduct — "

"No, Henry. But I do apologise."

"Pray spare yourself. Tell me rather — why you wished to see me again?" My lady's busy hands grew still and looking up into the dark face above her, she spoke in voice scarcely above a whisper:

"To beg you . . . for the last time, Henry, to be your noblest self. Forego your cruel vengeance, give up this duel, — forgive, pray forgive me any hurt I may have caused you in the past . . . do not harm those I love more than life. . . . Make me grateful, be the man I can remember in my prayers, the man I can most truly honour and — "

The soft, pleading voice faltered, died upon a gasping sob, for Mr. Willoughby-Gafton was laughing gently and, so laughing, spoke:

"Oh, Charmian, you do it admirably well, voice, tone, look and gesture all are perfect; yes, you play the rôle extremely well. But, my dear soul, you are out of place, the setting is entirely wrong and jars confoundedly! Those smiling cherubs jeer you, the roguish Cupids mock, Dame Venus up yonder flouts — and Victor — our pink and passionate Vicomte would — giggle, I fear. And, speaking of him, the gallant creature bears my letter to your spouse to-night, appointing the time and place of our final meeting."

"The . . . final . . . meeting!" she echoed, whispering. "Oh, Henry, have you . . . no mercy?"

"Had you in the old days, Charmian? And pray, how is Sir Peter? Well, I trust?"

"Yes . . . thank God!"

"Excellent! One wonders where he keeps himself. Not in the soft seclusion of this voluptuous nest, I judge?"

"No!"

"Precisely! The good Sir Peter would be ridiculously out of his element in this coquettish bower. But there are others . . . the fascinating Victor, for example, will be quite at home here — indeed he was, I believe, very lately?" My lady started, almost guiltily, and glanced up at her mocking questioner with look of quick dismay.

"How, how did you know?"

"What matter?" smiled Mr. Gafton with scornful glitter of sharp, white teeth. "He visits you here, it seems?"

"He has done so, once or twice."

"Exactly! And this brings us to the object of my visit."

"What do you mean?"

"Victor!" Here Mr. Gafton paced restlessly to and fro again while my lady sat mute and with face averted. "Yes — Victor!" he repeated and laughed stridently.

My lady rose and crossing to the carved mantel, leaned there close beside the cherub door and addressing Mr. Gafton over her shoulder, questioned him adroitly, speaking now in French:

"Pray, Henri, what of Monsieur Victor?"

Pacing slowly after her, Mr. Gafton halted where he might behold her face and when he answered, spoke in French also:

"Sacred Heaven, Charmian — but surely you are aware of his most vile reputation! And yet, I understand you actually stopped your carriage in the Bois to speak with him . . .

suffered him to ride beside you, and all Paris *regardant!*"

"Yes, Henri."

"Astonishing! May one venture to enquire why?"

"Does this concern you, Henri?"

"Not the least in the world, of course. Yet, considering your impeccable virtue, Charmian, remembering all your calculated modesty and icy propriety in regard to — my very humble self, I am curious . . . your sudden friendship for this notorious libertine, — to be with him is infamy for any woman of honour."

"Why, then," she murmured, "I must endure such infamy."

"Good God! And why?"

"Because I desire the Vicomte's help so bitterly."

"His help — his? Astounding! Why, in the name of heaven, choose such as — he?"

"Perhaps because he is your friend, Henri."

"Not so, my poor soul! I have no friends and want none. Victor is merely a means to an end, a — let us say, professional associate. I find him useful now and then — no more. But how

on earth may our little Victor aid Charmian,
our Lady Vibart? And — what shall be his
price?"

"But, Henri . . . what do you mean?"

"Dear creature, why effect an innocence so
stupendous? I mean frankly what shall be the
so helpful Victor's reward, guerdon or fee —
the *quid pro quo?* Our little Victor is one whose
services must be paid for and not lightly, believe me. . . . How, Charmian, are you silent?
Will not answer? Cannot? Then, in the name
of all that is purely innocent and spotlessly
chaste, explain at the least how he can aid you
and why you make choice of this brutal satyr,
this small, infinitely unpleasant French fellow?"

"Because," she answered, almost whispering, "because, Henry, I understand he can ex-
ert such influence upon you as will make it impossible for you to refuse my plea."

"Did he . . . did Victor tell you so?"

"Who else?" said she in the same hushed
voice.

"Ha, then — death of my soul, the fellow
lies!" cried Mr. Gafton passionately. "The

small, vile dog deceives you to your own misery and despair! For I tell you . . ."

And now the expected outburst came: scorn for her blind folly and bitter, scoffing denunciation of the Vicomte — his viciousness and utter, soulless depravity; in the midst of which tirade my lady, watching the cherub door expectantly, saw it open suddenly. And then upon the threshold stood the Vicomte, five feet odd of incarnate fury and murder.

"Ah — ah, Monsieur Henri," he sighed, "you speak, oh, very loud and — I have the ears!"

Mr. Gafton glanced at him, looked at Charmian's shrinking form, and laughing, set elbow upon the mantel and leaned there. The Vicomte tripped lightly into the room, folded his arms and nodded.

"Type of English pig!" he lisped. "Species of an animal most vile!"

"This small, infinitely unpleasant French fellow!" repeated Mr. Gafton gently.

So they faced each other, these two, the little, upright Frenchman and the big, graceful, lounging Englishman, surveying each other with such looks as had daunted many an unfortunate ere now, — the glittering deadly menace of unswerving eyes that had shaken many a pistol-hand, unnerved many a sword-arm and been the precursor of sharp death so often.

Now lolling thus, Mr. Gafton laughed for the second time, whereupon the Vicomte instantly leapt at him, cane upraised to smite, — but out shot a long arm, the cane was wrenched from him, snapped asunder and tossed out of the open window, all in as many seconds.

"And now, Monsieur le Vicomte," said Mr. Gafton, gesturing lazily towards the door, "be good enough to depart lest I be troubled to toss you after your cane."

The little Vicomte clenched passionate fists, crouched to leap again, gnashed his teeth and — controlled the impulse.

"To-morrow, Monsieur!" he hissed. "To-morrow — it is understood!"

"To-morrow, ah, perfectly!" answered Mr. Gafton, smiling contempt into those deadly, china-blue eyes. *"Au revoir,* Monsieur, until — to-morrow."

And when the Vicomte's quick, short steps had died away, Mr. Willoughby-Gafton strolled to the window and leaned there, staring down into the sunny garden. Then he laughed for the third time.

"Artful witch!" he murmured. "Oh, beautiful clever demon! I'm no match for your feminine tricks and cunning. . . . I never was. So to-morrow I shall probably slay our Victor, sweet Madame Charmian; yes, it has come at last by your contriving. But first — ah, Charmian, be sure of this — I shall certainly shoot your idolized Sir Peter! And so, thou dear, detested soul, farewell!"

Thus saying, he turned in slow and leisured manner, took hat and gloves and without further word or glance sauntered out of the room, closing the door gently behind him.

Then, uttering a broken, inarticulate cry, my lady sank weakly upon her knee beside the ottoman, head bowed between outflung arms, hands plunged deep amid the cushions. . . .

"Hush, Charmian! Oh, what is it? Hush, my heart's dearie — there now, there!" And yielding her shuddering body to the comfort of Miss

Janet's strong arms, Charmian spoke in horrified whisper:

"Janet, my hands . . . oh, my hands! God forgive me, there's blood on them! And yet this . . . this was the only . . . Other Way! Ah, let us hurry from this hateful place . . . this vile little house — come!"

CHAPTER XVI

TELLS HOW MR. GAFTON LISTENED TO A SONG

"ROBINET, my old one," yawned Mr. Gafton, lolling back in the much-worn armchair to thus contemplate more at ease the rich wine in his glass, "how many years have I held thee in bondage dire, — how long hast slaved to my will, Robinet?"

"Twelve!" answered Bob, scowling at the very elegant riding boot he was in the act of polishing. "Twelve years and more, sir."

"Only twelve?" murmured Mr. Gafton sleepily. "It seems much longer than that to me."

"Ar — and to me!" growled Bob. "A precious time longer — to me, it do!"

"Why then, here is news shall of a certainty delight thee, — attention, my cabbage! Behold, there is just a very faint possibility that the days of thy so grievous servitude may find sudden termination, the secret of thy so guilty past be secret only to thyself, and thyself free as air, my old grimly one, as a sunbeam, — as bird on bough."

"Sir," quoth Bob, turning the gleaming boot dexterously this way and that, "I don't twig. And, what's more, when you *tutoyers* me, it generally-allus means as you think I've done summat wrong or not done summat right and you're a-going to blow me up for it. So what I says is — what now? If it be on account o' me being out s' late last night — "

"Not so, my old debauched one, I blame thee not, no, no. It is, in effect, no more than that Fate may suddenly free thee of this thing of astonishing contradictions that calls itself Henri Willoughby-Gafton. To-morrow, my Robinet, the dear Victor and I go out together at last."

"Eh? Go out, sir? A dooel? You and the Vicomte? Well, — blow my dickey!"

"Sacred heaven!" sighed Mr. Gafton, shuddering languidly. "How deplorably vile can be our English tongue! However, to-morrow I shall certainly kill the dear Victor; this goes without saying. At the same time you will, my cabbage, perceive there is a bare possibility that the dear Victor may also kill me."

"Love us!" exclaimed Bob, very nearly dropping the boot. "He's a mortal good shot!"

"He is, my Robinet — against ordinary antagonists — a deadly marksman. But will he shoot straight when he knows that I perhaps shall shoot even straighter? 'That,' my old one, as the bard hath it, 'that is the question.' I should be willing to lay odds that he will not. None the less, the bare possibility remains that to-morrow I who now speak may speak nevermore but in silence rise . . . or sink to 'that bourne from whence no traveller returneth — ' *et cætera.* It thus behooves me to make such small preparations as I may. But, in effect, what? To draw a will with little or nothing to leave would be a wearisome futility . . . my animal, do you attend?"

"Sure-ly, sir! But — jest to think! You and the Vicomte! At last! Well, love me eyes and limbs!"

"Be silent, thou!"

"Very good, sir! Only — seeing as this matter be a bit serious-like, being a case o' life and death, as you might say, — why not talk English, sir?"

"So be it, Bob," said Mr. Gafton, sipping his wine with the pleasant deliberation of a connoisseur. "I suppose the prospect of death, sudden and sharp, is a fairly serious business to ordinary mortals, poor wretches, — but not to me . . . having so little to really lose and devil the soul to grieve for me. And so —" Mr. Gafton yawned.

"Well . . . but," quoth Bob, leaning down to breathe hard on the boot he had suddenly remembered, "if you should 'appen to be, — well, popped off . . . I shouldn't exackly sing for j'y, nor yet dance, sir."

Mr. Gafton troubled to turn and look at Bob's grimly sober visage.

"No," he murmured, "damme but I don't believe you would! And 'pon my soul, Bob, you're so sturdily English in spite of your French moustaches, that . . . hum . . . you're about the only thing, alive or dead, that I have any faith in."

"Sir, you never told me as much afore."

"Because I never troubled to think of it before."

"No, you never troubled yourself about nothing nor nobody, sir, — not you!"

"But I did, Bob, oh, I did! I have troubled myself quite damnably about — myself. . . . Hair thinning on the top! Graying at the temples, confound it! Wrinkles, Bob! Advancing years! Old age! Decrepitude, — the lean and slippered pantaloon! The solitary ancient, hoary and helpless, to die in the gutter, sans hair, sans teeth, sans — ha, the devil — not for me! Rather go out of life a man with strength and faculties alert to meet and combat . . . what is to be! Eh, Bob?"

"Ar!" he nodded. "I reckon!"

"Well then," continued Mr. Gafton, refilling his glass, "should I, the improbable happening, be — popped off, I leave you heir to all I die possessed of . . . trinkets, clothes, oddments and — what not."

Bob Meadows, having finished polishing one boot, set it down very precisely and took up the other.

"Sir," said he, without looking up, "you fair . . . as-tonishes me!"

"I begin to astonish myself, Bob. However, should I shuffle off this mortal coil, all that is now mine shall be yours with the sole exception of this ring," here he held up one hand, that deadly right hand, to show the emerald ring that graced it. "I should like you to give this to Lady Vibart and tell her — " the lazy voice paused and was silent so long that Bob glanced up at last with the question:

"What must I tell my lady, sir, — if so be — "

"Nothing, Bob! No, not a word, — say nothing."

"Very good, sir."

Here silence again except for the sound of Bob's busy polishing brush.

"How much of this wine is there remaining, Robert?"

"About two dozen or — " said Bob, glancing sharply towards the door, as in the lobby beyond, the cracked bell jangled harshly.

"That I fancy will be Monsieur le Colonel Santerre. Go see, Bob."

It was indeed that ferocious person who, scowling very portentously, marched into the room, flourished off his hat and bowed with an ominous *empressement*.

"Monsieur!" said he.

Mr. Gafton troubled himself to rise, returned the bow, yawned and sat down again.

"Monsieur?" he murmured.

"Monsieur," quoth the Colonel, stiff in the back as a musket barrel, "on behalf of my principal so esteemed, Monsieur the Vicomte — "

"Colonel," sighed Mr. Gafton sleepily, "be of the briefest. What says our gallant little Victor?"

"Monsieur will permit that I say my principal, Monsieur Victor, Vicomte de — "

"Colonel, in a word, — where does our small Victor suggest that I shall pleasure myself with his killing?"

"Monsieur Henri, he begs you will honour him by naming your weapon, *épée* or — "

"He shall choose, Colonel, all's one to me. But where do we meet?"

"Monsieur, behind the little *auberge* of the 'Good Man' by the wood this side Passy. You know it, I think?"

"But certainly. I remember it was there he shot and killed a young English officer of artillery last year. Also our Victor has an old,

tumble-down chateau thereabouts, I think.
. . . And to-morrow, of course."

"Perfectly, Monsieur, to-morrow at — sunset."

"Sunset, my Colonel? Now I protest you surprise me extremely! Why the delay? Why not in the morning, at his usual time? Six o'clock is our Victor's lucky hour, according to our Victor. Then wherefore this delay so remarkable?"

"Monsieur, it is that Monsieur the Vicomte has to-morrow an affair of the most pressing, but yes. It is understood? It is then agreeable to yourself, Monsieur, to-morrow at — sunset?"

"Of a certainty. Any time to-morrow I shall be quite charmed to give myself the joy extreme of accommodating Monsieur the Vicomte how he will, but for good and all! And now, my Colonel, you may remove yourself."

"Monsieur Gafton!" snarled the Colonel, scowling.

"My Colonel?" murmured Mr. Gafton, smiling.

"But your friend, Monsieur, your second? I would meet him. I demand to behold him —"

"Do so! Bob, stand up. My second, Colonel, shall be Robinet here."

"Ha, thunder!" exclaimed the Colonel. "Would you mock . . . would you make the foolish jibe?"

"Though not to-day, Colonel."

"But, Monsieur, death of my soul, — a servant!"

"And an Englishman, Santerre! Also, — remark me, sir, — as quick on the trigger and sure as myself — almost! Also you will notice he possesses eyes, — two, my Colonel! Now depart; your flourishes and empty gasconading weary one."

The Colonel glared ferociously, twirled his moustachio, swallowed hard and — took himself away.

"To-morrow . . . at sunset!" repeated Mr. Gafton musingly. "At sunset, did you mark that, Bob?"

"Ar, I did, sir!"

"Well, what do you think of it?"

"Very rum, sir. I never knowed him to fight
of an evening afore."

"Bob, it is so . . . ah . . . remarkably rum
that, knowing our Victor as we do, I think it
behoveth us to tread warily, not to say stealthily, that is to say — you shall! Yes, you shall
stalk our Victor, lurk upon his path, creep on
his footsteps, for there is some devilment afoot;
then you shall keep an eye on him and learn
precisely the meaning of this so pressing en-
gagement."

"Very good, your honour. But what I'm
a-wondering is, — why go all the way to Passy
when the Bois is so much handier — or say —
the ramparts or — "

"Well, but he has a house of sorts at Passy,
Bob."

"Ar, but sir, you don't think as he means to
make sure o' you, — a shot from cover, acci-
dental-like-for-the-purpose, eh?"

"Hum!" quoth Mr. Gafton thoughtfully.
"You raise an interesting factor, Bob — psy-
chology. For if our Victor is only half as sure
of his own final extinction as I am, he might
endeavour something of the sort. Victor has a

strong objection to dying and he never was a sportsman. Ha, the point is worth consideration. . . . However, you will be there and armed, Bob, and should any such trifling irregularity happen . . . my death from ambush, say, or even a wound, you will instantly shoot down our Victor as I shall announce to all and sundry so soon as we take our ground."

"And are you so very sure and sartin as you'll . . . end him, sir?"

"I haven't the faintest doubt of it."

"And are you . . . as sure-ly sartin as he won't . . . get you, sir?"

Mr. Gafton, refilling his glass, seemed to ponder this question, then glanced suddenly up at the dingy ceiling as from regions thereabout came a faintly sweet, childish voice singing an old-world, very familiar air.

Mr. Gafton set down his newly charged glass untasted and with gaze still fixed, spoke in strange, muffled voice:

"Why, what . . . Good God . . . what's the child singing?"

"Only 'Barbary', sir. I've been larning her to sing it in English — "

"After all these years . . . and why now?" exclaimed Mr. Gafton almost pettishly. "Confound me — why? Robert man, I knew a child once; she used to sing that song . . . years ago . . . I was a boy then . . . very young and innocent! . . . A pretty, old-time song! . . . Call her down, Bob, — the child. Call her here!"

"What . . . my little Nan, sir?"

"Certainly, my ass! Who else is there to call? No — do you fetch her, — go!"

"Why, so I will, sir, though she . . . she don't cotton to you, d' ye see, scared o' you she be — "

"Go bring her down here, man."

Slow-footed and unwilling, Bob strode heavily up the narrow stair to his attic and presently returned with the child throned in the haven of his powerful arms.

"Here she be, sir," quoth he, clutching her to his broad chest, "ar, — and her little 'eart a-beating like a small drum, so I'll — "

"Put her down, man, put her down. I'll not eat her!"

Scowling and more unwilling than ever, Bob

set the child upon her little dainty feet and with his hand upon her bright hair, stood regarding his master under drawn brows; while Nanette, trembling a little, looked at this grand gentleman from whose approach she had fled many a time and who had scarcely ever troubled to look at her until now.

So for a long moment they gazed on each other, the man and the child; then Mr. Gafton reached out his hand, speaking in voice so altogether strange and unexpected that Bob stared and the child forgot to tremble.

"Nanette, my little one," said this so altered voice in softest French, "wilt thou come hither to me?"

Very slowly she went to him and into that large, white hand laid her own small fingers; and in this same moment, as if all her fears were banished by the gentle clasp of this hand, she smiled up at him; and then, to Bob's stark amazement, she was seated on his Governor's knee.

"Wilt sing again thy song — to me, little one?"

"But yes, sir," she answered, "though it is in

the English and the words very difficult."

"No matter, sweetheart, I shall understand."

So, with Mr. Gafton's arm about her too-slender little body, the child sang the song another child had been wont to carol so many years ago:

"In Scarlet town where I was born
There was a fair maid dwellin'
Made all the lads cry — Well-a-day,
Her name was Bar-baree Allen.

"All through the merry month of May
When green buds are a swellin',
Young Jimmy Grove on his death-bed lay
For love of Bar-baree Allen.

"So slow and slowly she came there
An' slowly she drew nigh him,
An' all she say when there she came,
Young man, I think you're dyin'."

The song ending, Mr. Gafton sat awhile, his arm still close about his little singer, his dark eyes staring on vacancy, while Bob fidgeted, took up a boot, looked it over, put it carefully down again and finally spoke:

"It aren't exackly what you'd 'ardly call a cheery song, sir."

"It's better than that, Bob! And this little Nanette of yours is better still . . . so young, so simply sweet and innocent! So very near the angels! It harrows my soul to think she must grow up, change and degenerate into . . . a woman perhaps like Barbara Allen or — one more soulless. But to-day she's a child. . . ." Taking Nanette's little hand he looked at it wistfully, kissed it and set her down. "Take good care of her, Bob, be good to her, Robert," said he, rising. "And now, my hat, my gloves and cane. I'll stroll abroad and look upon the world a while."

"Nan," quoth Bob, shaking his head so soon as his master had gone. "I never see the Governor kiss ee afore. I never heard him speak so gentle afore and . . . I don't like it! No, I . . . do . . . not like it, my pretty, . . . not nohow!" And Bob shook his head again and more gloomily than ever.

CHAPTER XVII

Tells of Mons. The Vicomte, His Scheme

Monsieur Victor, Vicomte de Villebois, was taking the air, a small, very elegant, most arresting figure, to be hailed, saluted and smiled upon wheresoever he pleased to go; for this truly redoubtable little gentleman being a person of such high spirit, sangfroid, insouciance and, moreover, of such joyous deadliness, few were they that cared to disregard him.

And yet this morning, despite the gay bustle of this wide and sunny boulevard, his usual gaiety was not quite so exuberant, his swaggering step scarcely so youthfully buoyant, his tasselled cane swung less jauntily and his modish hat perched upon his sleek head at a less raffish angle.

At least, so thought Bob Meadows, judging with the assured knowledge of long association, as he followed amid the joyous bustle of this merry throng, dogging the small elegant, unseen and with the grim relentlessness of a pursuing fate that cannot be escaped or shaken off.

To a famous café came they, the followed and the follower, where beneath wide striped awnings the *beau monde* (and the *demi*) sat about small tables to laugh and chatter, sip and nibble while busy waiters flitted to and fro; to one of these sure-handed, quick-footed servitors, Bob signalled furtively with eloquent fingers, whereupon this same waiter nodded almost imperceptibly, while Bob edged himself unobtrusively amid the cheery stir and bustle and so got himself into a certain corner remote and shady and there seemed to vanish.

Thus, after some while, to a table in this same corner the waiter ushered Monsieur the Vicomte who, seating himself thereat, was presently sipping his absinthe, wholly unaware of the sharp eyes and keen ears that attended his every look and gesture.

So Monsieur the Vicomte sipped at his glass and, feeling himself here removed from the chance scrutiny of curious or admiring glances, became by degrees less and less the gaily smiling, too youthful elegant and more and more the haggard, care-racked man; his chubby person seemed to slouch, his china-blue eyes widened, his full rosy lips, instead of cherubic pout, showed flaccidly loose, — indeed Monsieur Victor seemed like one who, gazing into the future, sees a ghastly and very dreadful vision. . . . Then the plump, gloved hands clenched themselves, the eyes narrowed, the lips became a pouting line and sitting back in his chair the Vicomte saw Colonel Santerre stalking towards him through the chattering crowd.

"You are late, my friend Louis, late, late, late!"

"But Victor — to good purpose," answered the Colonel, seating himself with a flourish. "I have seen Papa Duplessis; it can be arranged, he will — intervene at the moment just. Behold, dear Victor, it is a matter accomplished!"

"Excellent!" exclaimed the Vicomte with all his wonted youthful gaiety. "And this *sacré* fellow, *le Bob?*"

"I shall myself attend to him in manner different but, for the time, effective . . . *Hola, garçon, un petit verre*. . . . But Victor, my dear old one, why run such risk condemned? For, perceive me, even Papa Duplessis may, having a tongue, talk — some day! Why not depend upon your own valour and skill so renowned? Victor, my friend, I ask myself — why not, wherefore, and why? It is not . . . ah, it cannot be . . . *sacrebleu!* You do not doubt yourself at last?"

"No, no, Louis. To doubt myself — ah, this is not possible for — I am Victor, me! For example, — I shoot — I kill! Always, my Louis, I kill! Is it not?"

"Dear Victor, I protest to heaven — it is! But — "

"So, — I kill. How then shall I doubt myself? The thing is of an absurdity! No, no, it is this fellow, this spadassin, this Henri, that I doubt. For observe, — when I fight, I make my man know I shall kill him of a certainty and behold — he is already dead! It is a matter of the soul, my old one, of the soul, ah! But now this Henri, this species of bull, this type of English beef, how shall he have a soul? Alas, it is not possible! For, regard, my Louis! He

knows I shall kill him and — he yawns! Sacred
name of a name, he gapes! We take our ground,
I look on him with the eye of the so certain
death and — he smiles! We level our pieces,
he stares into the muzzle of my pistol that cannot miss and — he nods with the head and aims
beneath my arm . . . at my very heart and
with a steadiness, oh, my faith, a steadiness the
most unshakeable! We fire — pim, pam! I kill
him perhaps upon the spot, but . . . oh, oh —
he also kills me of a certainty. I am no longer
alive . . . *oh, la, la* — upon my feet I am
dead! Name of a name, — it is a catastrophe!
And I am the corpse, my Louis, solely because
he is as the fish, of the blood so cold, ah — of an
iciness! Well, I kill him — oh, yes; but — behold, I am also dead, — which must and shall
not be, ah — no, no! For by sweet, smiling,
rosy Venus, I prefer so much to remain alive,
is it not? My God, it is! . . . And aha — behold! Over there! A nymph of a shape seduc-
ing! Come, my comrade, so good and faithful,
let us follow!"

So up started the Vicomte incontinent and,
with hat as raffish, cane-swing as jaunty and

step youthfully buoyant as ever, he set forth in chase of beauty, his stately jackal stalking at his heels.

"Well," quoth Bob, when he had watched them out of sight, "here's to warn the Governor . . . of all the chicken-'earted, lily-livered . . . well, blow me tight!"

Speeding home, he found Mr. Gafton dawdling over his breakfast to whom he unburdened himself forthwith.

"Why, this was expected, my Robert — almost! . . . Our dear Victor's hypnotic eye! His famous death-stare! Well, I'm hardly an hypnotic subject, Bob. To-night our Victor will be extremely dead."

"But where, sir?"

"At the *auberge* of the 'Good Man' at Passy."

"But, sir — "

"To Passy we shall go, my Robert, but with an escort. You shall hire some of your thuggish rascals to our protection, *les apaches,* that fellow Jules we used once before and one or two other like murderous gentry. See to it! And now as to the really important matter.

Explain to me what is the so pressing business that keeps our Victor until sunset."

"Why, sir, I — dunno."

"Eh? Why the devil not?"

"Well, you see, sir, me hearing this cur's trick they was for playing you, I come a-running and — "

"Then you will instantly go a-running, my ass! You will search all Paris until you find the Vicomte. You will track him till you discover what other knavery is afoot, then you will come a-running your very best and let me know. Is it understood? Then — off with you."

CHAPTER XVIII

How Charmian Denied Peter for the First Time and the Last

It was as she stepped from her carriage in the wide inn yard that my lady heard a sudden hubbub . . . rumbling wheels . . . racket of hoofs . . . a hoarse shout:

"Charmian!" And well knowing this voice, she clasped and wrung her hands, closing her eyes as if suddenly faint, while Miss Janet, in the act of alighting, started suddenly back again and gasped:

"Lord . . . Lord ha' mercy!"

Roused by this, my lady braced herself for what was to be, she opened her eyes, steadied her shaking limbs, sobbed once and became her competent and most purposeful self.

"Janet," she hissed fervently, "don't move and — not a word!"

So she turned and, approaching the scene of this sudden uproar, beheld a hackney-chariot with a hatless, tousled gentleman halfway out

of its window, a dusty, rumpled, fierce-eyed
gentleman who strove in the grip of two uni-
formed law officers.

"Charmian!" he cried again. "Thank
Heaven, it is you, my dear Heart. . . . I
thought you were in England. . . . Now, pray
tell these officious blunderers who I am — for
upon my soul I — "

"Pardon, Madame," said a third police officer, stepping suddenly between my lady and
the speaker, "but this man there, of the violence
so desperate, you recognize, you know him —
yes?"

My lady stared at her husband with exactly
the right degree of amazed and shrinking abhorrence to carry conviction and shook her
head.

"No — ah, no!" she murmured faintly.

"Ohé, Jules! Gaston!" cried the officer to his
comrades, "I was right, my old fellows; the
man is mad, of a certainty!"

"Eh?" cried Sir Peter, leaning farther out
of the coach window. "My dear, what's all this
about? They talk so confoundedly fast! What
are the fools saying?"

"Ah, beware, madame!" cried the officer, throwing out a protecting arm. "He is of a ferocity extreme, this fellow here, a ferocity *veritable!*"

"Indeed, I can well believe it," she sighed, shrinking behind that protecting arm. "Tell me, Monsieur the officer, when . . . how . . . where did you take him?" And upon this arm of protection she laid a small, tremulous hand.

Now this officer was young, very gallant and smart, despite sundry marks of recent combat, and now, looking down into the beautiful eyes upraised to his, and very conscious of the delicate hand upon his arm, he twirled his moustache and spoke full-chested:

"Behold, Madame — I am on patrol with my comrade, Jules, yonder, when we hear sounds of conflict. — We rush! We arrive and perceive this so mad fellow making the fight most desperate with his keepers. Ah, Madame, my faith — he kicks with the foot! He smites with the fist! He curses! He swears! He rages! He makes the disturbance terrific! But no matter — instantly we leap, Jules and I. We roll! We strive and — behold, we take him!"

"Ah, Monsieur, such bravery! But why do you bring him here?"

"Ah, Madame, that is the folly of my comrade Jules, for I say the man is mad, Jules says he is only drunk, and he himself protests he is an English gentleman; he demands we bring him here; he says in this hotel lives his son — "

"But, Monsieur, you never believe him, you?"

"Not I, Madame, no, no! But my comrade Jules he is of the thick-heads. So here we bring this madman and here he spies yourself, Madame, and is so mad to say you are his wife — "

"Charmian!" cried Sir Peter impatiently. "My dear soul, why all this confounded chatter? Tell the fools to let me out of this at once."

"Do not fear, Madame, we have him fast!" said the young officer, glancing down at the hand that had clenched itself upon his arm, "a madman of the maddest! Beyond all doubt."

"Beyond doubt!" she repeated.

"Charmian," cried Sir Peter, louder than ever, "good heavens, why don't you speak?"

"And as I say, Madame," murmured the

young officer, viewing that little hand as if he would have kissed it, "as I say — of a ferocity!"

"Then you will take him away . . . you will keep him safe . . . very safe and secure?"

"Oh, never doubt it, Madame."

"But you . . . you will see they treat him gently . . . oh, very . . . very gently?"

"How — a madman of such violence, Madame?"

"Please! Ah — for my sake! Promise me, Monsieur."

Now hearing the pleading voice, beholding all the supplication of these lovely, eloquent eyes, feeling it, moreover, in the gentle pressure of these slender fingers, the young officer flushed, smiled, saluted and inflated his chest.

"Madame, upon my heart and soul — I swear!" said he; then wheeling smartly, "Hola, Jules, Gaston," he called, "to the Bureau — forward!"

"Charmian!" cried Sir Peter in hoarse amazement, "eh . . . what . . . are you mad . . . am I mad? Charmian . . . good God . . . d' you mean — "

Hoofs clattered, wheels rumbled and, as the

coach lumbered away, my lady turned and stumbled blindly towards the inn, but ere she reached it the faithful Janet was beside her.

"Oh, Janet, Janet," she sighed, "did you hear? Did you see? His troubled voice . . . his dear face! But I did it — oh, I did it! Pray God they keep him secure . . . just a few hours longer."

"Charmian, you're ill!"

"No, no, a little faint. And . . . so dreadfully tired — "

"And no wonder! Will I get ye a sup o' brandy?"

"No, a little water." They had reached the wide porch before the inn door where stood a broad settle, and here my lady sank down, her weary head bowed upon tremulous hands. But hardly had Miss Janet left her than she glanced up to see the Vicomte bowing before her, hat a-flourish.

"Alas, dear Madame," said he breathlessly, "Your son heroic, Monsieur Richard, with an audacity superb he seeks but now Monsieur Henri — ah, but haste, Madame, haste with me or they fight and your son so gallant becomes

the corpse. They will fight immediately — this
hour! But go now with me . . . courage, dear
Madame, for I am Victor. You will not permit they fight and, sacred name, they shall not!
— I, your friend, I, Victor, say so. Only haste,
Madame, haste to prevent this deadly meeting.
. . . See, I attend you my carriage — behold!"
And even as he spoke, a light *calèche* drew up
at the door. Shaken and distressed, hardly
knowing what she did, Charmian suffered him
to aid her into the vehicle. . . .

Now as they swung out of the inn yard, she
caught a glimpse of Bob Meadows, she saw
him halt to stare, saw him flourish an arm
wildly, heard him shout — and then they were
out in the busy street, and yielding to this
strange inertia that seemed to numb her every
faculty, she closed her eyes awhile; but warned
by some feminine instinct, she opened them and
beheld a face very near her own, lips that
smiled, eyes that watched her . . . and reading something of their evil, she cowered away,
then reached desperately for the door. But her
hand was gripped fast, these pale, sinister eyes
drew and held her, and the Vicomte spoke:

"To-morrow, Madame, thanks to you, it is possible I may die. Ah, well, to-night, my goddess, I am alive, and to-night — "

Charmian screamed, but a small, vicious hand stifled her and she knew the deeps of terror and despair before she sank into a merciful oblivion.

CHAPTER XIX

GIVES A VERY BRIEF DESCRIPTION OF A RIDE

SIR PETER, being the indomitable soul he was, so bestirred himself — and others, officers and officials high and low, with divers gentlemen of the Embassy and Consulate, that long before sunset he was back at the inn of the Soleil d'Or, fuming with anger, highly indignant and extremely mystified. Nor was he soothed to learn that "Mesdames were out driving, monsieur his son was away riding and monsieur his son's gentleman was abroad taking the air."

Cast thus upon his own resources, Sir Peter strode off to the stables, selected a likely saddle horse and presently rode grimly forth in quest of Mr. Willoughby-Gafton.

Thus it befell that Bob Meadows, walking a mettled animal to and fro before his master's lodging, heard the clatter of other hoofs, saw a horseman ride briskly into the courtyard and beholding this same grim visage, stood agape.

"Is your master in?" demanded Sir Peter, drawing rein.

Staring round-eyed, Bob gulped and before he could find speech, Mr. Gafton appeared, booted and spurred and heeding Sir Peter no whit, leapt into the saddle.

"Sir," began Sir Peter, "I desire — "

"To the devil with your desires! Out of my way, sir!" cried Mr. Gafton impatiently.

"Certainly not, sir," retorted Sir Peter, serenely determined, "until you have heard the explanation I — "

"Curse your explanations, sir! Give way or I'll ride you down."

"You may try, sir!" quoth Sir Peter, barring his way. "But you shall hear what I mean to — "

In went Mr. Gafton's spurs and his spirited animal cannoned into Sir Peter's horse so violently that both riders were nearly thrown; hoofs clattered wildly, sparks flew, and before Sir Peter could check his beast's furious plunging, Mr. Gafton was out and away.

"What the devil!" exclaimed Sir Peter in angry amazement. "Is the fellow mad?"

"Why, sir," answered Bob, scratching his chin, "I dunno. But, ye see, the Vicomte's off wi' your lady —"

"Eh . . . my lady? D' ye mean Lady Vibart? Good God, d' you mean — my wife?"

"Ar!" nodded Bob. "Her! Tricked 'er into a chaise, 'e did, sir, and is driving away wi' her 'eavens 'ard, your honour —" Sir Peter stooped suddenly from his saddle and pinning Bob by the collar, glared down into his unwinking eyes.

"Is this — true?"

"Ar," nodded Bob, imperturbable as ever. "Ar — true as — death, sir. That's why my Governor's gone a-gallopin' arter 'em —"

"You say the Viscount. What Viscount? His name, man his name!"

"The Viscount de Villebois, sir . . . golden 'air — there aren't much of him, sir, but what there is, well — it's rank pizen —"

"Where has he taken her?"

"Well, I reckon he'll make for his old chateau at Passy, sir — leastways my Governor's took that road and I'm a-coming too, ah — and not alone —"

Sir Peter's powerful horse reared beneath goading spurs, bounded across the courtyard and steed and rider were gone.

The streets at this hour were thronged, but Sir Peter threaded his way amid the teeming traffic at speed so reckless as evoked indignant shouts and cries from men who drove and folk who walked, but on he spurred unheeding. Once or twice he checked to enquire his way, then forward he rode again, fast and furious as ever. Thus soon he had left the great city behind, houses gave place to trees and wide fields where labourers straightened weary backs to watch the madman ride.

Trees and fields, clustered cottages, solitary farmsteads, darkling woods, — uphill and downhill with rhythmic beat of wild galloping hoofs. . . . And so at last, topping a rise, he beheld a moving speck afar that grew to a pigmy horseman, — to a man on a raking grey steed going at an easy canter; thus Sir Peter, riding at such furious pace, was soon near enough to see this horseman was Mr. Gafton who now, hearing his approach, turned in the saddle and recognized him, scowled and, in that moment, swung his horse about, barring Sir Peter's way.

"Sir, what are you about?" cried Sir Peter angrily.

Mr. Gafton merely laughed and cantered on before at the same leisured pace. Sir Peter swerved, essaying to pass on the near side. Mr. Gafton swerved also, still barring his advance. Sir Peter swore. Mr. Gafton laughed again. Three times thus Sir Peter endeavoured to pass and thus three times Mr. Gafton checked him.

"Scoundrel, let me by!" cried Sir Peter. "You know my hurry."

"Fool, there is no hurry!" retorted Mr. Gafton. "I am giving Madame Charmian time to more properly appreciate her rescue — "

"Damn you, Gafton, she is my wife! Will you let me pass?"

"Curse you, Sir Peter — no! He is my enemy!"

"Pull over!" cried Sir Peter. "Make way, or by God I'll ride you down!"

"Do so," laughed Mr. Gafton, "and there will probably be no rescue — " With voice and spur, Sir Peter urged his snorting animal forward but as he did so, Mr. Gafton turned in the saddle with levelled pistol . . . a deafening report, a puff of smoke, and Sir Peter's rearing steed plunged to earth, pitching his rider headlong. . . .

And, after some while, Sir Peter scrambled painfully afoot to find himself beside his dead horse upon a barren, desolate road.

Nevertheless, bruised and shaken though he was, he stumbled resolutely forward, — bemused, half-blind with blood, yet indomitable as ever.

CHAPTER XX

The Other Way; Which is the End of Charmian's Scheming and Naturally Ends This Narrative

MY lady sighed deeply, shuddered violently, opened her eyes and instantly closed them again, for muttering over her was a wizened old woman and beyond this aged crone an aged man who gaped toothless jaws, and beyond him again the Vicomte, who stamped and raved in a pale, tremulous fury.

"Malediction!" he exclaimed pettishly. "Rouse her, my old Jeannetton! A thousand devils, — wake her, Jeanne! To kiss a woman who swoons, it is without savour; ha, sacred name of a name, I scorn it — yes! So rouse her for me this instant, I say!"

The old woman muttered to the old man, who shuffled hastily from the room, — this little dim, panelled chamber that had but one small, heavy door armed with bar and bolts fashioned in a wilder age, — this my

lady glimpsed through the curtain of her
lashes. . . .

They slapped her hands, they fanned her,
they bathed her temples — without the least
effect: sal volatile, vinegar, burnt feathers, she
endured them all and continued to swoon with
an unshakeable pertinacity, while the Vicomte
stamped to and fro, filling the air with his peevish, high-pitched revilings until, pausing suddenly, he smote himself upon the forehead.

"Aha — brandy!" he cried. "Cognac! Eau-
de-vie! Come Jacques, thou species of insect,
dost hear?" And he sped away, the old man
hobbling after.

Now hardly were they gone than my lady
sat up suddenly on the broad settle and, gasping as in mortal terror, pointed up at the one
small lattice high in the panelling.

"Sacred heaven!" she whispered. "Ah, behold — see yonder!" The old woman turned
in swift alarm and in that moment was seized
by desperate hands, propelled across the floor,
bundled out of the room and the door slammed
to behind her; the rusty bolts squeaked, the
heavy bar creaked into its massive sockets and,

sinking upon her knees, my lady leaned there, her pale cheek pillowed against the stout old door, her lips murmuring soft yet very fervent prayers.

Presently as she crouched there, came thud and patter of footsteps on the stone flags without; then was a frenzied shouting, while fists pounded and feet kicked furiously on the stout timbering. And contrasting this strong door with those small, vicious feet and little, deadly hands that beat and smote in such passionate futility, Charmian began to laugh, — shrill, wild laughter that rose and swelled high above all other sounds. Reeling to the settle she sank down and laughed until she wept — sobbing until she could weep no more; and lying huddled thus, very spent and weak, she trembled now because of the brooding hush, the ominous, all-pervading silence. . . . At last upon this dread stillness rose tread of heavy feet . . . a jingle of spurred heels . . . voices. Up she rose and creeping to the door, crouched there listening. She heard the Vicomte's voice, in the distance, shrill and fiercely threatening, followed by a lazy, sneering laugh, mocking and familiar. . . . Footsteps and voices were drawing nearer.

"Very well!" cried the Vicomte. "It is enough! You shall die, species of dog — ah, but slowly, yes — you shall suffer — aha!"

"Type of a small monkey, you chatter!" drawled Mr. Gafton's mocking voice. "Come, little ape, the orchard shall be a place quite admirable, — ah, no, not behind me, Monsieur the Vicomte, we walk side by side — so! You show a little pale, I think . . . ah, well, you shall be paler beyond a doubt . . . after — " The footsteps turned aside, the two voices, the one full and even, the other piping and querulous, died away. . . .

In the pause that ensued, the long-drawn, deadly stillness, Charmian sank to her knees again, clasped hands against the door, head bowed upon them, while fierce tremors shook her. And thus she crouched there . . . waiting . . . waiting for these two men to take this Other Way, this path she had lured them into, this way that led them even now to death and destruction. . . . Desperately she strove to pray but could not, her sick mind racked and

thralled by the dreadful thing that was to be
. . . out there in the orchard . . . that place
of shady trees and tender grass where stood
two men facing each other with eyes of murder. . . . And this was the end of her own
scheming! . . . She cowered lower, straining
her ears in a dreadful expectancy, but heard
only the heavy beating of her own troubled
heart. . . . She began suddenly to count —
one . . . two . . . three . . . four — ah, God,
at last!

A sudden, sharp report . . . a long, long
moment of breathless suspense and then a second explosion that rang loud and was gone.

Ah, merciful God — and this was of her contriving!

Sinking upon the floor, she lay there moaning fitfully, then checked her breath to listen
in swift panic.

Footsteps again! But whose? Feet upon the
flagstones outside . . . some one was coming!
. . . but who? Which of these two men yet
lived? The feet came on, treading with soft,
short steps . . . nearer . . . nearer yet. Fingers scraped and fumbled at the door. . . . A

hand knocked. Then a voice spoke, half-whispering, curiously repressed:

"Your road is . . . clear. You may . . . open the door."

"Henry?" she cried breathlessly. "Oh, Henry — is it you?"

"Myself, yes, for a . . . little while."

With shaking hands and yet wholly unfearing, she drew bolt and bar, opened the door and recoiled.

Mr. Gafton stood upon the threshold, one hand braced against the wall, the other pressing a handkerchief to his mouth.

"Henry?" she whispered. "Oh, are you — hurt — in pain?"

"A little," he murmured. "Congratulations . . . Madame Machiavelli! Also our Victor is . . . completely dead, and as for me — " he laughed, choked, and the handkerchief at his mouth became dreadfully stained. Then Charmian's arms were about him . . . and so she brought him to the wide settle; but when she would have sought and tended his hurt, he shook his head.

"I'm . . . beyond . . . troubling about!"

"Let me see," she pleaded; "ah, let me see what I can do."

He smiled and shook his head again.

"Your work . . . is done, madam, for . . . egad . . . so am I!"

Here lolling back, handkerchief to mouth, he gazed up at her with his old look of mockery until, as though stricken by something in this look, she sank upon her knees, gazing up into his anguished face with swimming eyes.

"Tears?" he whispered. "Good God!"

"Henry," she sobbed, "see, I'm kneeling to you as you vowed I must, kneeling to beg you'll suffer me to do what I can . . . . to ease your pain."

"Oh, no, Charmian . . . it's through the lungs . . . I . . . have it at last . . . I'm going out. I . . . wonder where."

"No — no," she sobbed. "Ah, no, pray God!"

"Yes, Madame. But . . . why grieve? Your Peter is . . . safe. On his way here. The fool would have . . . got himself killed . . . so I . . . shot his horse . . ."

"Oh, Henry!" she whispered, and clasped

his nerveless hand. "Dear Henry, is there . . . nothing I can do to show — "

"Yes! Come nearer . . . it's growing . . . dark . . . night for me very soon, so . . . come . . . nearer — " Now, seeing how his tall form swayed and drooped, she took him into the tender comfort of her arms, pillowing his heavy head upon her shoulder.

"Ye Gods!" he murmured, smiling wanly up at her. "So here I am . . . at last, Charmian . . . for just a little while, and then . . . slumber."

"Henry dear," she whispered, as she bent above him, wetting that pallid face with the passion of her grief, smoothing the thick hair from his clammy, pain-creased brow, "can you, will you — forgive?"

"A . . . silly question!" he gasped. "Dear, I . . . loved you better . . . than I knew . . . Charmian, you said . . . that you'd remember me in . . . your prayers. Will you . . . now and then?"

"Yes . . . always, Henry."

"Then . . . Charmian . . . sing me . . . to sleep. Night is falling."

"Oh, Henry . . . how can I?"

"The old song . . . Barbara Allen . . .
the cruel minx . . . and Jimmy Grove . . .
the poor . . . the poor . . . fool! I've time
for one . . . verse . . . sing!" And so, blinded
by tears, she sang brokenly:

> "In Scarlet town where I was born
> There was a fair maid dwellin'
> Made all the lads cry — Well-a-day
> Her name was Barbara Allen."

"Poor Jimmy! . . . A fool," he gasped, "to
die . . . for a woman . . . poor . . . old . . .
Jimmy! Now it's coming . . . the darkness
. . . stoop to me . . . girl. Will you . . . kiss
my eyes . . . this weary world . . . from my
. . . sight. . . ."

Very tenderly she obeyed him and with his
failing eyes thus gently closed, he sighed:

"'And now . . . to . . . sleep. . . .'"

And thus, with Charmian's cherishing arms
about him and weary head pillowed on her
bosom, Henry Willoughby-Gafton passed on
to a greater life, perchance.

In a while, kneeling beside this stilly form

ennobled and dignified by death, she prayed for him and for herself, while the evening shadows deepened all unheeded.

Until was a sound of hasty feet and a hoarse voice that cried a little wildly:

"Charmian! Oh, Charmian!"

Then she arose and met Sir Peter in the stone-flagged passage.

"Dear Heart," said he, folding her in eager arms, "you are safe . . . unharmed? The Viscount lies stone-dead out yonder . . . but you . . . he . . . he did you no hurt?"

"No — ah, no, my Peter," she answered, nestling closer in his fervent embrace. "Only I am sad . . . very sad and tired, Peter — dreadfully tired — "

"But what of Gafton? The scoundrel shot my horse and — "

"Hush, Peter, — hush, my dear. Come with me."

So together they entered the little chamber and stood there very silent a while.

"He was a man who died for you, Peter, and for my sake. . . . He was a man I feared and — hated, God forgive me! For, oh Peter, — in-

deed he proved greater . . . nobler . . . than
I thought — "

"Why then," said Peter gently, "he assuredly
is so yet."

"Yes," murmured Charmian, stooping to
touch that pale, serene face, "ah, yes, for that
which is truly good lives on for ever."

Being come out from the old chateau, this
place of death, of ruin and decay, Charmian
shivered and turning suddenly, clasped Peter
in her arms, clinging to him like a frightened
child.

"Take me home!" she whispered. "Take me
back to the dear, quiet country things . . . to
home and — England. For oh, my Peter, I am
more . . . ah, much your humble person now
than ever!"

END

DATE DUE

GAYLORD			PRINTED IN U.S.A.

card 2

828
F23c   Farnol, Jeffery
AUTHOR

            Charmian, Lady Vibart
TITLE

DATE DUE	BORROWER'S NAME
F 4 '38	Margaret Mary Phillips
Mr 18	

828
F23c

CPSIA information can be obtained
at www.ICGtesting.com
Printed in the USA
BVHW050010090223
658191BV00002B/143